by

Chris Redfern

Copyright © 2015 by Chris Redfern

All rights reserved in all media. This book or any portion thereof may not be reproduced or used in any manner whatsoever without the express permission of the author.

This book is entirely a work of fiction. The names, characters and incidents portrayed within are the product of the author's imagination. Any resemblance to actual persons, living or dead or events or localities is entirely coincidental.

ISBN: 1518776973
ISBN-13: 978-1518776977

For Connor, Wil and Harry.

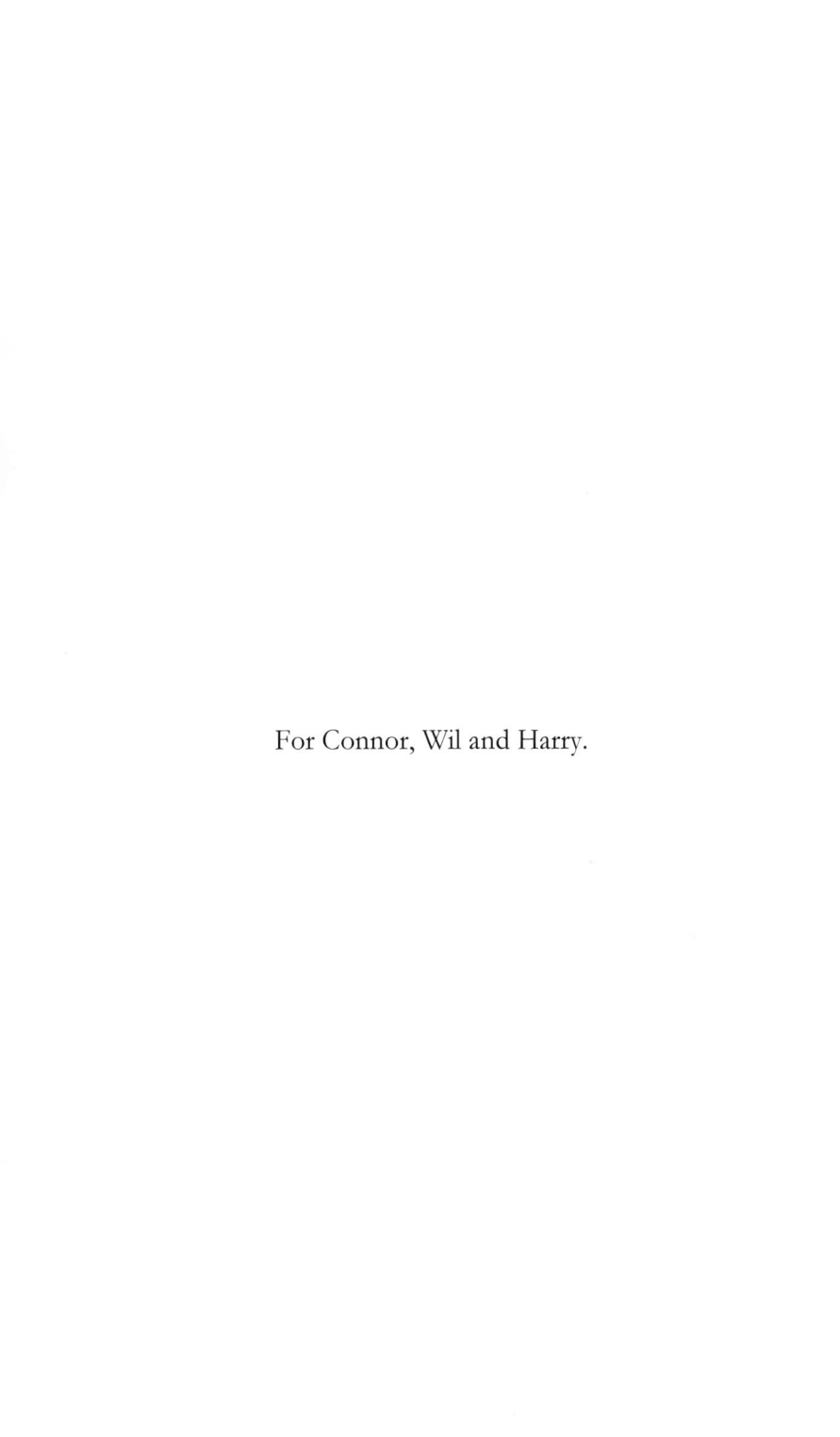

CONTENTS

Acknowledgments	i
Chapter One	1
Chapter Two	8
Chapter Three	17
Chapter Four	29
Chapter Five	38
Chapter Six	48
Chapter Seven	58
Chapter Eight	71
Chapter Nine	83
Chapter Ten	88
Chapter Eleven	102
Chapter Twelve	110
Chapter Thirteen	115
Chapter Fourteen	122
Epilogue	133
Afterword	136
Biography	140

ACKNOWLEDGMENTS

Cover Artist

I first met Trystan Mitchell in early 2014. We'd been paired up together to work on a story I'd written for the quite brilliant comic anthology, *The Psychedelic Journal of Time Travel*. We hit it off straight away, especially when it transpired that we'd both grown up in the same town of 'sunny' Bolton.
His style of artwork is quite simply stunning. It manages to be both expressive, highly detailed and extremely character driven – a perfect match for my kind of writing. Since that first story, we've since collaborated on several other projects and there's more in the pipeline.
It's been an honour watching him put together this wonderful cover and I can only hope it goes some way to showing off his talents to a wider audience. More of Trystan's artwork, his extremely clever paper toys and all of his contact details can found on his website www.thebigfootstudio.com You can also follow him on Twitter @inkfunnel

Editor

Alison Williams provided both a professional and timely service in her capacity as Editor. She went above and beyond my initial brief, ensuring not only the accuracy of the words, but also suggesting valuable plot changes along the way. Alison's website contains a list of her editing services, as well as links to her own historical novels and can be found here
www.alisonwilliamswriting.wordpress.com

CHAPTER ONE

Downtown Chicago was bustling with people enjoying the unusually warm, early summer weather. Frank smiled as he watched his wife and daughter dancing about before a mime artist, trying their best to make the 'statue' laugh.

Jolted from his thoughts by ice-cream dripping down his hands, he called his family over. Aayla took her ice cream and, with a grin, set to work catching the rapidly melting drips.

"Thanks honey," said his wife as she took hers too. "You know, I bet you could make him laugh."

"Oh?"

"Just tell him one of your jokes," she answered with a hint of a smile, before she too busied herself with her ice cream.

"There's something wrong with my jokes?" asked Frank looking shocked. "Seven years of marriage and you hit me with a bombshell like that!"

"It's probably best out in the open."

"Well, in that case I want a divorce."

"I call evidence from the prosecution," said Lara, using her ice-cream as a microphone. "Sergeant Reynolds, did you, or did you not, attempt what might be described as a 'joke' at the Speakman's party last week?"

"Err, yes your honour."

"And did you, or did you not, have to explain the punchline?"

"Objection your honour. At least one person laughed."

"Sure, that woman who was eight months pregnant. She laughed… right before bursting into tears and leaving the room."

"That wasn't my joke… it was your soufflé." Lara stuck her tongue out at him, which, covered in ice-cream as it was, made Frank laugh even more.

"Okay, come on you two," he said with a glance at his watch. "The funfair opens at three and I know you're desperate to go on the hyper-coaster."

"No we're not," replied Aayla. "You're the one who's not stopped talking about it all day." Like most seven-year-olds, she hadn't yet grasped the concept of sarcasm.

"She has a point," said his wife with a grin.

"Okay, so I might have mentioned it a few times," said Frank. "Anyway, I'm pretty sure Kal will understand me, even if you two don't."

Lara rolled her eyes and gently patted her stomach. "Jeez, how many times do I have to tell you, we're not naming our baby after some comic book character… and besides, I'm pretty sure it's a girl."

"What? Three against one!" cried Frank, grasping his head and almost dropping his ice-cream in the process.

The three of them laughed and joked as they made their way along a busy Main Street towards the fair and Frank couldn't remember feeling any happier; 2110 was turning out to be the year things were finally started to go right.

Suddenly a scream shattered the tranquility of the day. It was quickly followed by the harsh sounds of crunching metal and smashing glass. Frank looked across the road to see that a hover car had gone out of control. It had rammed itself into the doors of a huge office building and several pedestrians appeared to be hurt.

"Frank…" began his wife, knowing that her husband probably wouldn't be able to stop himself if people needed help. It was one of the things she loved about him most. "You're not on duty. I'm sure the CPD can handle this without you." But before he'd even had time to move, the driver of the wrecked car had climbed out. He was wearing a full face balaclava and was dressed in dark, combat clothing. *What the hell's going on?* thought Frank, a multitude of alarm bells now ringing in his head.

When the driver started to run, for some reason Frank knew he had to stop him.

"Hey you…" was all he managed before the car exploded, taking him, his family and most of the block with it.

"How is he?" asked the young woman, who, despite her age, probably held more qualifications than the majority of people at St Mary's, Chicago's newest and largest hospital.

"Not great," replied the nurse as they walked down the corridor together. "He has no family now; it's tragic."

"He's refusing robotics?"

"Won't even consider them."

"Then hopefully I can help."

"Perhaps," answered the nurse, stopping before a closed door. "Look, I know you mean well Dr Brown, but…" The nurse looked up at the taller woman and, despite her kindly manner, her eyes now had an edge to them. "I also know who you work for. Try not to upset him please."

Helena Brown tried not to let the shock show on her face. She'd studied Frank's history in detail and knew he was a former Special Forces soldier turned policeman. The way he looked now, it was hard to visualize him as the same man she'd seen in the photographs. All of his limbs were gone. Only four heavily bandaged stumps remained and the rest of his body was a mass of dressings and bruises. Although Helena had seen people recover from worse, she knew there were other wounds from this that would never heal.

"Frank," began the young woman slowly. "My name's Dr Brown and I'm here to help you."

Frank ignored her and, propped up against a pile of pillows as he was, continued to stare at the opposite wall. Helena took off her glasses and rubbed her tired eyes. She'd hardly slept last night, her mind too active to fully relax. Was she doing the right thing? Was she really here to help this man… or simply to further her own career? She brushed such thoughts aside, just as she'd done before, and tried a different tactic.

"Okay, so maybe I'll come back another time. My fault Frank, I should've guessed it's too early after losing your family."

"I didn't lose them. They were murdered," came the brusque reply.

Helena didn't let her smile show. She knew it was a low blow bringing up his family, but she needed him to listen. What she had to propose could change his life forever and she wasn't about to be ignored.

"Look Frank, I'm with Cyber-Tech Solutions. We're the world leaders in robotics, advanced technology and…"

"I said no robotics," he replied, now turning to face her.

Helena saw nothing but anger and suffering in his eyes.

"I know that Frank, which is why I'm offering something different."

"Will it bring my family back?" asked Frank, his eyes distant.

"No… I'm afraid not. But it'll give you a chance at life again and perhaps something more."

"Like what?"

"Revenge."

Frank's eyes flashed with barely concealed longing and Helena felt things tipping her way.

"Frank, my grandfather's Johan Larrouy and he owns Cyber-Tech. I'm here with an offer to help you get that revenge."

"Go on."

"Cyber-Tech funds a special project called COLT - Cyber-Organic Limb Trial and, as you've probably

guessed, it's about more than just robotics."
"I already said…"
"It's about weapons," she interrupted.
"Weapons?"
"Yes Frank, weapons."
"Okay Dr Brown, I'm listening."

CHAPTER TWO

As usual, Frank felt groggy coming round after the anaesthetic. The stimulant injection helped, but even after this, the fifth and last of his complicated surgical procedures, he had woken up feeling weak and disorientated. He looked around and saw he was back in his own room, the one he'd been given on his arrival at the COLT labs almost two weeks ago. *How time flies when you're having fun*, he thought with little humour. All of this served one purpose, the chance to avenge his family. That's why he took the pain and that was why he awoke each day with some more of the world's most technologically advanced hardware attached to him.

"How's the arm Frank?" asked Dr Brown, sweeping into the room.

Clinical and straight to the point as ever, he thought. Here was a woman so driven by her work, he'd yet to see her smile. Frank knew she was under a lot of pressure to make this work, but whether that pressure was self-induced or came from higher up, he couldn't be sure. Certainly he'd yet to see any sign of Johan Larrouy, the man Helena said was her grandfather, but that didn't mean he wasn't watching Frank's every move. Frank looked down at his arms. The left seemed identical to the right, which itself had only been fitted a few days ago. Each was constructed of a smooth, metallic silver material. He flexed his new fingers, pleased to see a response akin to flesh and blood.

"Still feels strange."

"It shouldn't feel that strange Frank. The nano-sensors are designed to send signals to your brain as efficiently as the human nervous system."

"I meant the robotics."

"You'll get used to them. It's what happens next that's a bit different."

A bit different? thought Frank. *She sure knows how to understate the facts.*

"And that's down to the thing you put in my head?"

"Yes, the Morphing Cortex will control everything."

Frank knew his robotics differed in a new and very experimental way from those fitted to amputees over the last few decades. The Morphing Cortex had been implanted directly onto his brain and would allow his new limbs to change - to morph into something else.

The Cortex itself hadn't been turned on yet, as Frank had been told he needed to wait until all of his new limbs were checked and fully functioning. But he could almost sense it in there, waiting.

"Flick the switch Doc, looks like I'm ready," he said, lifting up his robotic arms and flexing them in turn.

"It's not that simple Frank. You don't just 'flick a switch'," replied Helena. "There's a mountain of data to be verified first. Now, how are the legs?"

With the last of his drowsiness leaving him, Frank swung his legs outwards to sit on the edge of the bed. Just like his arms, they were constructed of solid but lightweight metal composites and, since their fitting a week ago, he'd already found himself with as full a range of motion as before. Perhaps more so. He felt no fatigue, no cramping, and, owing to the power of the motorised muscle system, there was impressive physical strength. Only yesterday he'd accidently crushed the rails on his bed by gripping them too hard. Technicians had quickly reprogrammed the feedback loop, making it more compliant with a normal human response, but Frank knew the strength was there. All this was remarkable, but it was what lay ahead that interested him.

"So tomorrow then?" he asked.

"Possibly," she replied. "This isn't something we can just rush into and the next stage is going to be pretty tough for you. Don't forget, you're treading new ground every day here." She attached a series of electrodes to his new arm.

"But will it work?" he asked.

"There's no reason to think otherwise."

"I'll be able to change their shape?"

"Yes, that's the whole point. The Cortex allows them to change organically. Your limbs will have the ability to morph..."

"…into weapons."

Dr Brown stared at her patient and took a deep breath. So far everything was going to plan, but

Frank's obsession with weapons and revenge would need careful watching. She bent down to check the join between flesh and metal at his shoulder. "The COLT project's come a long way Frank," she began, "and you're about to take the next step. Although the actual morphing will start small, it'll expand with time. Remember, you're not the first person to do this." Happy with the way the arm appeared to be healing, she looked him in the eyes. "For the record, you're the forty-fifth subject to get a Morphing Cortex."

"I guess that makes me COLT-45."

"That's your COLT designation, yes."

"Just like the gun." He smiled.

"Get some rest Frank; it's going to be a busy day tomorrow."

Frank watched her go. He was willing to play their games, at least, for as long as it took to get what he wanted. After that… well, then there'd have to be some new negotiations.

As the doors to the COLT labs closed behind her, Helena felt her shoulders slump. She was pushing herself too hard and the strain was starting to show. *Why the hell did I mention his COLT designation?* she thought angrily. She wasn't eating or sleeping enough and now, on top of all of that, she'd started to question her own judgement. Helena had always been careful to avoid any emotional attachment to her patients and with good reason as it turned out. But with Frank it was different. She felt sorry for him, especially after all he'd been through. However, there was something else. She owed Frank her life. Admittedly it was many years ago now and he obviously didn't remember her. *This is how I repay him?*

After what he did for me…?

Thoughts like that could compromise the entire project and so she quickly banished them from her mind. There were things Frank Reynolds didn't, couldn't, know about the COLT project; or he'd never agree to the next step.

Helena sighed. She'd been immersed in her work for so long, it had simply taken over. It was all she thought about from the moment she awoke, to the time she fell exhausted into her bed each evening. Looking back now, it seemed unreal to think all this had grown from a small but interesting idea she'd had whilst at college. That idea had ballooned, mostly through her own hard work and perseverance, into something that could actually herald the next evolution of robotic technology. Granted, her family's wealth had helped her somewhat along the way, but the fact remained that this was something she'd done by herself.

The basic idea was simple. In much the same way as a human brain sent signals to the various muscle clusters, a specially designed interface of nano-processors, one that worked in direct conjunction with the brain, could be used to send another type of signal. In this case, a very specific type of signal; one that didn't just ask for movement, it also demanded a change of state. A limb was told not only to bend or lift, but to become something else, to form something different. That was cyber-organics, or morphing as it had become more commonly known and there were few people in the world with the same depth of knowledge about the process as Helena Brown.

For decades, morphing had remained unworkable, mostly due to its inherent instability. Early trials showed that if a limb was given a signal to morph, it would do so. But then it would do so again and again and again and all in the space of a few milliseconds. The end result was extremely unstable and more often than not, highly explosive. However Helena had found a way to solve this problem. She'd created her own interface, a Morphing Cortex, which, when grafted to the correct part of the brain, could manage this change in a safer way. The Cortex ensured the correct signal was sent and then, using a complex string of mathematical programs, strictly controlled all subsequent changes. The future looked bright for Dr Brown and the decision was made to begin testing her Cortex in earnest. COLT was given its own laboratories within Cyber-Tech. It had its own budget, its own staff and Helena was immediately promoted to project manager. Everything pointed towards this being the biggest breakthrough in robotic technology for centuries. But then they discovered a flaw.

As ever, Helena tried to block the memories from coming, but it just wasn't that easy anymore. She'd gotten too close to the project, back when it had first started and hopes were high. It had all begun with the arrival of Jango.

Jango was a young, male chimpanzee and the first of the COLT subjects. Not knowing any better, Helena had immediately formed a bond with the creature, one which was to be her undoing. Even after his limbs had been replaced with robotics, Jango was still trying to please her.

She'd never had time for pets and so with Jango, she'd suddenly found herself feeling something new. Unlike most people in her life, Jango wasn't interested in wealth or important family connections. He'd just wanted to be loved and she couldn't help but return that emotion. It had made her feel special... feel wanted.

Hating herself for dwelling on the past, Helena couldn't stop herself from picturing Jango's face that day, the day she'd first turned on the Cortex. Pain, quickly followed by confusion, a brief moment of accusation and then finally, emptiness. It had taken Jango less than twenty seconds to die.

Ever since that day, finding a way to overcome this flaw had become Helena's obsession. It was what drove her to exhaustion every day and what kept her awake at night. She'd almost given up on finding an answer, but then, out of the blue, came Frank Reynolds. His circumstances fitted the COLT model precisely and Helena knew she'd been thrown one last lifeline. Tonight, she'd discover if he'd been worth the effort.

After Dr Brown had left, Frank lay on his bed thinking over what she'd said. *If he was COLT-45, then where were all the others? What about COLT-1, or COLT-2 or COLT-44 for that matter? What had happened to them?*

Turning his head, he looked towards the old fashioned, two-dimensional photograph of Lara and Ayla that sat in a wooden frame next to his bed.

"Goodnight my angels," he said quietly, before closing his eyes and waiting for the nightmares to begin.

Helena arrived early the next morning and, like

Frank, she looked like she'd hardly slept at all.

"Morning Frank, sleep well?"

"No," he replied simply, swinging his legs off the bed.

"Look, I won't lie to you; it's going to be a tough day mentally as well as physically. If you're not up for…"

"I'm ready," answered Frank. "Besides, how bad can it be if forty-four other people have managed it?"

"That's great," she replied, turning away from him.

She was fast, but not fast enough for Frank. His time in the police had taught him many things, not least the way someone's eyes could speak volumes. *So Dr Brown, there's something here you're not telling me.* Frank knew he'd have to tread carefully if he wanted to discover more.

"So…" continued Helena, scurrying about the room, starting up the recording and testing equipment that lived in there with him. "No headaches? No problems with vision? Nothing unusual to report?"

"No. Should there be?"

"Sometimes the Cortex takes a little while to adjust," replied Helena, still with her back to him.

"Well, I guess when we turn it on we'll know for sure."

"Frank," she said, turning to look at him. "It's been turned on for almost two hours now."

"What? Why the hell didn't you tell me?" asked Frank. "What if I'd changed my arm into a nuclear missile or something? Surely you…"

"Frank," interrupted Helena. "The decision was made to activate your Cortex when you were asleep. That way, any neuro activity would be at a minimum and…"

"But I didn't sleep."

"Well you must have. Our instruments recorded…"

"Seems your fancy instruments are wrong Doctor. I wasn't asleep. I was in a meditative state; it's what I use to keep the nightmares at bay."

"But…" began Helena looking flustered, "…that'd mean a successful conscious activation…"

"I don't care what it all means. Does the Cortex work or not?"

Helena stood with her arms crossed, looking at Frank thoughtfully. He found he didn't particularly like it.

"The Cortex is working perfectly. So the question is, are you ready for the next stage?"

Frank tried not to let his excitement show. His questions about the previous COLTs lay forgotten. His Morphing Cortex worked, and that meant weapons.

"Okay Dr Brown," he said with a smile. "Let's do this."

CHAPTER THREE

"That's it... keep going Frank," said Helena.
"Easy... for... you... to ... say," came the grunted reply. Frank was straining hard and had sweat running down his face as he continued to force the change. But it was working. He had one of his new robotic arms held up before him and it was slowly changing. He continued to stare at the place where, only minutes before, one of his metallic fists had been. Now there was a blade, about six inches in length and sharply pointed, and it was still growing.

This was his second day of testing and Frank finally felt like he was getting somewhere. Yesterday's efforts had produced little in the way of morphing and a lot in the way of exhaustion. However Helena seemed pleased and, for the first time ever, Frank had seen her smile. *Was there another side to this cold and clearly work-orientated woman after all?*

Today she'd promised him results and Frank had to agree, she'd been right. After the disappointment of yesterday's exertions, he'd listened carefully to her advice. She'd explained how he'd be better 'requesting' the change instead of just trying to force it. This was apparently the whole point of the Morphing Cortex. The way it interacted with the brain should be natural; it shouldn't be seen as some kind of mechanical addition. It had to be a part of him, as if it'd always been there. Try that, Helena had promised, and the signals would flow more naturally.

The blade before him was now eight inches long and Frank had fashioned it with razor sharp edges. However, the strain of this continued morphing was something he was now struggling to deal with. Frank could feel himself tiring by the second.

"That's it," he panted, breathing heavily. "That's all I can do."

"Okay Frank, that's good work. Tomorrow we'll…"

"AAARRRGGHHH!"

Suddenly his head exploded in agony.

"Fight it, Frank!" she shouted over his screaming, desperately trying to pin him down whilst avoiding his flailing weapon. Frank was vaguely aware of people rushing into the room, before his vision blurred and darkness came as a blessing.

"So you're saying my brain… what, tried to reject the Cortex?"

"Yes Frank," replied Helena sounding tired. She was in a chair beside him and taking notes as she watched data scroll across the screen of her tablet. "It's an area we've always had trouble with."

"And you didn't think to mention this before?"

Helena sighed and looked up at him. "Okay,

maybe we should've talked about this. It's just…"

"You didn't want me to change my mind."

"Not exactly. Look Frank, the way you responded to the initial tests was just so positive. With the others…"

"Yes, about those others…"

"What matters," interrupted Helena quickly, "is that you did it. You morphed your hand into a weapon."

"Sure I did," replied Frank, raising his reformed metallic fist before him. "But what use is that when I'm out cold?"

"It won't be like that next time Frank. The Cortex is still active and that means that your brain's beginning to accept it. The pain comes because it's linked to your nervous system and that needs time to adjust too." Unplugging her tablet, Helena rose to leave. "Anyway, you'd better get some rest. Let me know when you're ready to start testing again."

Frank looked from his fist towards the young doctor. "I'm ready."

"But…"

He began to concentrate. Slowly his hand began to morph, to melt once more into a different shape, one that started to stretch and narrow. It took a massive amount of effort, but within moments, he'd once again created the long, sharp blade. *Well,* he thought to himself, *that bit's getting easier. But… here comes the fun part…*

The pain hit hard, but this time he was ready. He gritted his teeth and fought the agony until slowly, very slowly, the pain began to subside.

"See…" he grunted, collapsing back onto the bed and dripping with sweat, "…piece… of cake...doctor..."

Helena watched as Frank drifted off to sleep, his blade automatically morphing back into a hand again. *Yes,* she thought with sudden and renewed optimism, *Frank Reynolds was exactly the person she needed to make COLT a success. Not only was he stubborn, brave and determined, but more importantly, he was the only one to have survived this far.*

"So Frank, you wanted to see me?" asked Helena, striding into his room. Today she wore a suit instead of her usual white laboratory coat, and looked like she'd just come out of a meeting. *Probably one about him*, he thought without much humour.

Frank was standing in front of the large fish tank. He'd asked for it a few weeks ago and, after a small battle of wills, Cyber-Tech had eventually given in. It reminded Frank of his old life, back when he had something to actually live for. He could still remember the look on Aayla's face and her constant stream of questions when he'd installed a tank at home.

"So why can't we put any fish in?"

"Because the water's not ready," Frank had replied, one arm up to his elbow in the salty water as he tried once again to build the reef.

"Looks ready to me."

Frank had laughed. "That's because you can't see all of the important chemicals living in there too. Phosphate, calcium, magnesium, the level of alkalinity... all those have to be just right before we put any fish in."

"Dad…"

"Yes princess?" he'd replied, crouching down and searching through the bucket that contained all his expensive pieces of reef rock. If he could just find one the right shape…

"It's fallen over again."

Frank had sighed and looked up at the tank. She was right. His carefully crafted reef had collapsed yet again. Resisting the temptation to throw the rocks across the room, Frank had instead carefully placed them back into the bucket.

"Tell you what. Why don't we try this again later?"

"Sure Dad. So what do you wanna do now?"

"Ice-cream?"

"Yey! Ice-cream!" She'd raced around the room with her arms in the air.

Frank had laughed. "So that's a yes then?"

"And as for you," he'd whispered, staring daggers at the fish tank, "don't go thinking you've won."

"Frank?" He was jolted into the present.

"Dr Brown," he began carefully as he turned to face her. "I've been here six weeks now and it's obvious my morphing abilities have peaked. I can make some lovely knives, but anything more complicated is proving impossible." Frank watched carefully for her reaction. Did she suspect he was holding his abilities back? In truth, Frank couldn't be sure himself. He'd recently started to feel he could morph further, perhaps creating something more advanced. But before he was going to do that, he wanted something back from Cyber-Tech; and not just a fish tank. Frank wanted the truth, and he'd decided now was the time to get it.

"You're doing great Frank and we've still…"

"I want to leave."

Helena suddenly looked very tired. "We talked about this already," she replied.

"Where are the other COLTs?" he asked suddenly, hoping to surprise her with the change of direction. It worked too. Once again he saw something in her eyes, something that told him she was holding back the truth.

"You know the answer to that too. We needed to keep you separate because…"

"Are they dead?"

Helena remained silent for a short time before answering. "Just remember why you're here, Frank," she replied and turned to leave.

"Oh, I know why I'm here alright and guess what… it's not for Cyber-Tech."

Helena stopped but didn't turn around. "Revenge is a dangerous state of mind Frank," she said softly.

Frank smiled and closed his eyes. "Right now Dr Brown, it's all I've got."

"Sir," began the smartly-dressed man, sitting before an array of screens in Cyber-Tech's main control room, "Subject's just left COLT." As Director of Security, Stefan Slade took his job very seriously. Which was why, as he steadily deactivated systems to let one of the COLT subjects escape, it all felt rather uncomfortable. Another reason, and perhaps the one making him sweat the most, was the fact that Johan Larrouy was standing behind him, monitoring his every move.

Slade ran an operational staff of one hundred and twelve people, but he'd chosen to do this job himself. It wasn't that he didn't trust his own men; he just knew that if Mr Larrouy wanted something done, it had better be done properly.

"Good," came the deep-voiced reply. "And he can exit the main gates?"

"Yes sir. After trying his card on the COLT doors, he didn't stop moving from there. He knows he's been spotted, but I guess he's just making a point."

"The guards, they're not going to be a problem are they?"

"No sir, they've been briefed."

Johan Larrouy nodded and, satisfied everything was going according to plan, turned to leave the Control Room. *And so Mr Reynolds*, he thought with a smile, *you have your freedom. Unlike my granddaughter, I'm inclined to think you'll learn more on your own.*

Helena was furious. Not only had Frank Reynolds escaped from COLT, but he'd been helped to do so by her own grandfather. She slammed the front door of her apartment behind her and threw her bags onto the floor. *All that time and effort… for what? Nothing!*

"Good evening Helena," said a disembodied voice. "Might I be of assistance?"

"I seriously doubt it."

"Well in that case, rest assured everything's in good order. Dinner's in the oven, you have two messages and I've let the cat out."

Helena paused in the process of taking off her coat. Sometimes having an apartment run by computer had its benefits.

"Sorry Jeevs. Feel free to ignore me, I'm just having one of those days."

"That's perfectly alright Helena. Are you sure there's nothing I can do to help?"

"Nah," she replied kicking off her shoes. "Just play message one."

"… *beep*… Hi Helena, it's Ross. Look, about that date next week, I'm afraid I'm going to have to cancel. Something's come up and …"

"Delete."

"Play the next message?" asked Jeevs.

"Might as well, today couldn't get any worse."

"… *beep*… Hello Dr Brown, this is Ruth Cobbe from Serenity. I know you're probably busy with work and everything, but… well, I think Nathan would really benefit from another visit. Obviously there's no rush, just… well, just think it over please, thank you… *beep*…"

Yup, it gets worse. Slowly, she walked over to the large piano that dominated her living room. Spread across its flat surface was a collection of old-style, framed photographs. Sitting herself down upon the piano stool, she reached for one of them and gently blew off a layer of dust. The picture showed a girl of about ten. She was sitting on the floor behind a boy half that age and had her arms around him. They were both laughing, full of the innocent and joyful pleasure of life. Helena could barely remember the last time she'd felt like that.

"Jeevs," she said, placing the photograph on the piano and putting her shoes back on again.

"Yes, Helena?"

"You have my dinner, I'm going out."

"I'm afraid eating is not something I've been

programmed…"

The rest was lost as she closed the door behind her.

"Dr Brown, thank you for coming," said the matronly looking woman who met her at the door. "Visits are so important for the continued…"

But Helena was no longer listening. Every time she came here feelings were unearthed that she'd rather keep buried and before she knew it, she was back in the past.

"I thought Nanny was picking us up from school?" asked Helena, climbing into the hover-car after her brother.

"Yes, well, your mother rang and asked if I could do it instead," answered Steve with a smile. "And besides, would Nanny take you to McDonald's on the way home?"

"McDonalds! Yeyyy!" shrieked Nathan, quickly strapping himself into his booster chair.

Helena smiled. It was hard not to like Steve. Although he was only her step-dad, he was Nathan's biological father and because she doted on her little brother more than anything else in the world, Helena tried hard to make their disjointed family work for his sake.

"Here you go Tiger," said Steve, turning to pass Nathan a comic book.

"Wow… you got me Shazam! That's my favourite, thanks Dad!"

Helena couldn't help but smile as her brother's

face lit up with joy. He'd always loved comics and, despite their mother's blatant disapproval, Steve always tried to sneak him one whenever he could.

The car journey home was only a short one and as they set off towards Overton Hill, one of Chicago's more affluent areas, Helena found herself daydreaming. It'd be Christmas soon and she hoped to get more upgrades for her Holo-Dolls. Every so often Nathan would interrupt her thoughts, shouting 'SHAZAM,' or another catchphrase from his comics, but she didn't mind…

"What the…?" began Steve suddenly.

Helena looked across at her step-father. She didn't know much about driving, but the way he was fighting the steering wheel didn't seem right and as the hover-car started to skid sideways, she found herself more frightened than she'd ever been before.

"Hang on!" yelled Steve.

"SHAZAM!" shouted Nathan.

And then everything went black.

Events that followed were never more than a series of tumbling, disjointed memories, lost amongst urgent voices and flashing lights. Nathan… was he asleep? Blood on Steve's face… the pain in her side…

However there came a day, about a month after the accident, that Helena remembered with startling clarity. She was alone with her grandfather in his office when he'd uttered the words that would forever change her life.

"Helena, this is going to be hard for you to hear, but your mother has decided to go away…"

"What do you mean go away?" she'd interrupted, already fighting back tears. "I don't understand. Go where?"

"I can't answer that Helena, because… because I don't know myself."

"So what's going to happen to me and Nathan?" she asked, tears now running down her cheeks.

"It's complicated, but…"

"No it's not," she sobbed. "It's not complicated at all. Steve's dead and Mom's gone away. So what happens to us?"

"I'm going to look after you."

"Nathan too?" she asked hopefully, but already knowing the answer.

"No, I'm afraid not."

"But why not? I'll help look after him. All we need to do is…"

"Helena," he interrupted softly, "it wouldn't be fair on Nathan. He needs to be somewhere special; somewhere they can take good care of him…"

"Dr Brown?" repeated Ruth, looking across at her with sympathy.

"I'm sorry," replied Helena, shaking herself from the past. "I just… well, never mind. Let's just go see Nathan shall we?"

"He'll be delighted to see you. He always is. It's been a while since you were last here, but I'm sure you'll find…"

Helena had once again stopped listening. Although Ruth Cobbe meant well, she always made Helena feel so incredibly selfish. *That's in the blood I suppose*, she thought with some distaste. Serenity had been her grandfather's idea and it was his money that had built it, but for Helena, it remained a painful reminder of the past. As she walked down the corridor with Ruth, she tried not to look too closely at the other patients. Most were physically disabled and all of them had been diagnosed with some form of mental problem or another. They all needed specialist care; care only a place like Serenity could provide. Helena knew that these were the lucky ones. They received the best treatment money could buy, but she also knew it wasn't really for them. It was always about Nathan and, with a deep breath, she walked into his room.

"Hello Nathan,'" she said as his tortured face turned towards her.

"SHAZAM!" came the uncomprehending reply.

CHAPTER FOUR

Frank Reynolds sat at the table in his small kitchenette and picked at the leftovers from last night's take-away. The micro-servos in his robotic arms hummed gently as he dropped the cold noodles back into the pot. He'd never quite mastered chopsticks and it seemed his new robotic fingers couldn't cope either. As ever, his eyes flicked up towards the wall opposite. Pinned across its surface was a sprawling collection of printed emails, maps and photographs, as well as dozens of other smaller, handwritten notes. It was an old fashioned approach to detective work, but it had worked for Frank in the past.

Since his escape from COLT six months ago, he'd used his time wisely. He'd managed to gather vast amounts of information about TALIR, the terrorist organisation. The name came from its motto: 'The Answer Lies in Revolution'. The group was infamous across the globe for its attacks on profitable western companies, as well as for running high profile media campaigns. However, the organisation itself was shrouded in secrecy and, despite strong ties to other anti-capitalist terror groups, exactly who bankrolled them was the biggest mystery of all.

If he was being honest, apart from all the information gathering, Frank had made little real progress in his quest for revenge. But the last six months hadn't been wasted, far from it. He'd spent a good many hours practicing and experimenting with his morphing and, overall, he'd been pleased with the results. In a way, Frank was glad he'd held back some of his abilities at COLT.

The door buzzer jolted him from his thoughts. In all the time he'd rented this apartment, he'd yet to have a caller.

"Door…View," he ordered and instantly the front door became transparent. He didn't recognise the two large, muscular men who waited outside, but he had a fair idea who'd sent them.

"Damn," he whispered, before moving over to the window. Frank punched in the key code and its shutters immediately began to motor open.

BBBBUUZZZZZZZZZZ.

"Coming…" he shouted towards the front door, which now showed the men with weapons in their hands. Frank eyed up the distance to the street below and somewhat belatedly wished he'd chosen a ground floor flat.

WARNING! – DOOR SYSTEM OVERRIDE! – WARNING!

As he heard the door slide open behind him, he made a decision and, with a small prayer, launched himself headfirst out of the window.

Frank fell quickly. The fact his limbs had been replaced with metal didn't help him win any battles with gravity, but at least he had a plan. He tried to ignore the fact he was plunging to his death and instead attempted to clear his mind. He focused on the task at hand, on what he needed his body to do, and, within his head, the Morphing Cortex attached to his brain began to communicate to his robotic arms. Slowly, but with increasing frequency, the cyber-organic material in his arms began to change. His hands formed into hollow exhaust pipes, forearms became compressor turbines and then suddenly, there was ignition. Flames burst from the end of each arm, narrowing into intense, burning cones of thrust and Frank felt his descent begin to slow. But it wasn't happening quickly enough. He was still plummeting towards the ground at an alarming speed and so, with a quick correction to the angle, he asked the jets for more power.

"Come on," he urged himself, "COME ON…!" As Frank strained for one last effort, he felt the jets respond, giving him the power he needed. Slowing rapidly and with only metres left to go, he finally managed to stop his fall. Extinguishing the jets, Frank dropped to the pavement and swiftly morphed his arms back to normal. At that point, the all too familiar pain hit home. More controllable now than it had been during those early days at COLT, it still felt like he was having rusty nails hammered into his head. This morph had been a big one and, unfortunately, the resulting pain was somewhat in proportion. It brought him to his knees and several seconds passed before he realized someone was standing next to him.

"Hello Frank," came a curt, female voice, slowly filtering through the pain. "We need to talk."

Frank recognised the voice and, slowly getting to his feet, turned to stare at Dr Brown with thinly disguised contempt.

"What? You guys miss me or something?" he asked without humour. It was then that Frank noticed the stretch limousine parked behind her. Its rear door was open and inside was the immaculately-dressed Johan Larrouy. Frank's wasn't surprised to see him smiling.

Frank slumped on the wide leather seats of the limousine and watched in silence as the bustling crowds flowed past its blacked-out windows.

"You shouldn't have left, Frank," began Helena angrily. "I could've helped you. The project was designed to…"

"Seems to me," interrupted Larrouy gruffly, "that Frank's learnt more on his own than he did in your labs."

Visibly stung by his words, Helena flushed and was about to object when a stern look from her grandfather silenced any retort.

With a sigh, Frank turned to look at the man opposite. They'd met only briefly during his stay at Cyber-Tech and for that he was thankful. Johan Larrouy was in his sixties, but looked about twenty years younger. A Chicago man born and bred, he was a big guy with a big personality and at that moment, it was his grin making Frank nervous. It was like watching a shark smile.

"I won't be a prisoner again, Larrouy,' said Frank, sounding more determined than he felt.

"I know that Frank," answered Larrouy. "So let me be blunt. I need your help."

"You need my help?" said Frank with a laugh, more than a little surprised at the way the conversation was going. "Now this I've got to hear."

Larrouy's smile vanished. Back was the man who'd built an empire from nothing. A man renowned throughout the industrial world for his aggressive corporate tactics and a willingness to take experimental technology to the cutting edge. Frank held his breath and expected the worst.

"Seen the news?" asked Larrouy.

"No, I…"

"This was two hours ago," he said, passing Frank a tablet running various media streams across its display.

"Another terrorist bomb?" began Frank. "Where?"

"Cyber-Tech offices in London. Twenty confirmed dead, over one hundred injured."

"My God," whispered Frank. The similarities to the explosion that had killed his family were all too apparent.

"TALIR have once again claimed responsibility and, counting the failed attempt in Singapore, that's three attacks against my company in one year. I want it stopped."

"What do you expect me to do about it?" asked Frank angrily, the freshly stirred memories cutting deep.

"I'm informed," began Larrouy carefully, "that there's a certain Russian company bankrolling TALIR."

"I seriously doubt it; but go on, who?"

"Cyber Corp Russia. They've been on the CIA's

Blacklist for years, mostly because of their links to other terrorist groups. But what I need is proof; proof CCR are behind TALIR and proof they ordered the bombs."

"Wait a minute," began Frank, leaning forward. "Are you seriously telling me the people who ordered the bomb, the people behind the murder of my family, are just some Russian businessmen?"

"Don't be so quick to dismiss the Russians, Frank. It's a different place to when you fought over there. In recent years most of their large companies have been bought by the Chinese and that makes them wide open to corruption."

"Corruption like TALIR?"

"Exactly. But the problem is I need to prove it and that's where you come in."

"But why me? You've got enough money to buy an army."

"Hear me out Frank. There's a very good reason I need your help."

"Yes, I bet there is. But guess what, but I'm not playing your games anymore Larrouy. You don't believe me? You want to test me? Go ahead." Frank raised his hands ready for the change.

"Okay Frank, calm down," said Helena. "We get the message."

The large man continued to stare coolly at Frank. He was not a man used to threats. "Look," he began, with a somewhat forced smile. "I'm not very good at asking for help, so I'll keep this simple. I'm offering you a sure fire way to get your revenge."

"Explain."

"Once I get the proof linking CCR to TALIR, I want you to lead the strike force and take them both out."

"Operating outside the law?" asked Frank, already knowing the answer.

"Naturally."

"And I get to choose my own team?"

"As long as they're from my own men, then yes. They won't disappoint you."

Frank sat back in the car seat, lost in thought. If all this was true, then surely it was the chance he'd been looking for. Whether he went in with Larrouy's men or not, that was unimportant right now; this was the best lead he had. For some reason there were alarm bells ringing in his head, perhaps because it all seemed, well, just a bit too convenient. Frank looked at Helena, but she was giving nothing away. No doubt his escape from COLT had slowed her illustrious career somewhat. No, she was no longer on his side, if she ever had been in the first place.

"Okay Larrouy, let's hear the plan."

The large man tried not to smile. If Frank wanted to hear more, he knew he was at least tempted and that meant there was a chance this outrageous plan might just work after all.

"In two days' time, Helena's got a meeting with the senior directors of CCR at their headquarters in Russia. It's a genuine business deal, above suspicion. You'll go with her and, once inside the building, find a way to get separated. From there, I'll remotely direct you to the company's mainframe, where you download the data and we get that proof."

"You make it sound easy," replied Frank. "But I still don't get it. Why do you need me?"

"The building's as secure as any of our facilities, perhaps more so. They deep scan everything that goes in or out and, if we're going to make this work, we need a way of getting the data out without anyone realising."

"And I'm that way?"

"Yes, we'll download the data straight into your Morphing Cortex."

"And they won't know?"

"Once in there, the data's completely shielded. That makes it undetectable."

"Don't you think they'll be a bit suspicious? I kinda stand out?"

"I've read your files Frank. Tell me, your Russian still good?"

"Yes, but..."

"Then you're Helena's translator."

"Okay, but what happens if I get caught?"

Larrouy looked at Frank with an intensity that was frightening. "I reckon you know the answer to that Frank. If you're caught, Cyber-Tech won't support you in any way and this conversation never happened. You'll be arrested, convicted of espionage and probably thrown into some Russian hellhole prison."

Frank wasn't shocked. He'd suspected as much anyway and Larrouy's revelation didn't change anything. He'd been given a chance, a chance for revenge and, right now, that was more than he could have hoped for. Obviously he didn't trust Larrouy and he couldn't work out why Helena was getting involved, but this was just too good an opportunity not to take. *Plus*, thought Frank with a sly smile, *with all that stolen data in my head, I'd be the one making the deals.* He probably wouldn't need Larrouy or his assault team. He could plan an operation against CCR himself and, after that, well, when he'd squeezed some information out of the Russians, TALIR would be next. Frank smiled at the thought.

"Okay, I'll do it," he said.

Larrouy grinned back. "I thought you would."

But Frank wasn't listening; he was too busy making plans of his own.

The limousine dropped Frank off at his apartment before returning to Cyber-Tech. It wasn't until it was pulling up before the building's front doors that Helena finally broke her silence.

"So what makes you so certain CCR are funding TALIR anyway?" she asked, turning to face her grandfather.

"I'm not," he replied curtly. "That's why I need the data, to know for sure."

"And you're not bothered that this is…well, all a bit dangerous?"

"It won't be for you," he answered, turning to face her. "Just concentrate on that meeting, Helena. Close the deal and you'll get your wish."

"I still can't believe you closed COLT. My work was a massive success; well it was until you let him escape."

"Back to that again? Keep pushing me and I'll find COLT a new boss."

"You wouldn't dare."

As Johan Larrouy left the car with a smile, Helena found herself wondering if she really knew her grandfather at all.

CHAPTER FIVE

As the supersonic jet began its descent into Russian territory, Frank stirred from a broken sleep. Dr Brown and her half dozen aides still sat by themselves at the opposite end of the luxury jet. Despite several attempts at conversation, she'd politely, but firmly, declined Frank's advances and continued to busy herself with paperwork. *She's still annoyed about me leaving COLT,* thought Frank with little sympathy. However, she wasn't the only one living with a few difficult truths. Despite the way they'd gone about it, Frank couldn't help but acknowledge the fact that Cyber-Tech had kept their promise. They'd given him his life back, exactly as they had said they would. Yes, his new robotic limbs meant he could live that life like the next person, but what of the promised revenge? *Patience*, he urged himself. If this mission proves successful, that promise was one step closer to being fulfilled. Had he honestly thought Cyber-Tech would provide all the answers? Frank remembered being so full of anger when he'd first arrived there, that that was exactly what he'd expected. Eight months on and the reality was somewhat different.

After his escape from the apartment window, Cyber-Tech now knew about the rocket jets, but what they didn't know was what else he'd managed to create. They didn't know about the weapons. Frank smiled at the thought as he looked across at Helena again. He watched her arguing with one of her aides about some detailing in the paperwork and shook his head. This Helena Brown was a very different person to the one he'd met nearly eight years ago and Frank found himself wondering if she even remembered him from that day. She'd never mentioned it, but it wasn't the sort of thing anyone would forget in a hurry. As Frank watched the wispy, white clouds zip past the plane's window, his thoughts drifted back.

"So what d'you think's going on in there Frank?"

Frank smiled at his partner. *How many times had he asked that now?*

"Probably not much. The hostages are safe... so long as nobody does anything stupid," he replied. The pair of them had been on cordon duty behind the Principal Arts Museum for several hours now and were still awaiting relief. Finlay was a good kid, but still something of a rookie and at times like this it showed.

"Anyway, I don't know why are we're even here," continued Fin. "They ain't coming out this way, it's a dead end."

"I hope you're right, because you're a terrible shot."

Fin knew Frank well enough now to know when

he was joking. He was still considered the new kid and being the butt of everyone's jokes was expected. "Look, here comes Bérnard and McCoote now." Two of CPD's finest were ambling up the back alley, obviously in no rush to take over from Frank and Fin on boring cordon duties.

"Hey guys," said Fin. "What's happening out front?"

"Well, the hostages have been brought out," answered Bernard, the chubbier of the two policemen.

"They have?"

"Yeah, in small pieces, all wrapped up with little pink bows…"

"Alright Bérnard," interrupted Frank with a grin. "Don't encourage his imagination. What's really happening?"

Bérnard shrugged his shoulders and adjusted the gun belt below his sizeable stomach.

"SWAT have turned up. They're going in."

Frank hoped this was just more of Walter's bluster, but he'd already guessed something like this might happen. The terrorists had gone into the museum well-armed and had taken hostages within minutes. They were well organised and therefore highly dangerous. More importantly, they'd certainly be ready for any rescue attempt.

"C'mon Frank, let's go see what's going on," said Fin.

"You guys heard who's in there?" asked Bérnard, examining his fingernails.

"Yeah, we heard. Hostages are a load of college kids."

"A load of college kids *including* the governor's

daughter."

"Christ..."

"That'll explain SWAT," said Frank. "This might turn…"

BOOM

"What the hell was that?" asked Fin.

"Some hero wanting to save the governor's daughter," said Frank.

"So whatta we do?" asked Fin.

"Why don't you guys just stay here?" said Bérnard. "Might be better if we went back out front again."

Fin waited for his partner to speak. Frank was like that, always thinking things through before making a decision. Although they'd been partners for nearly a year, he still knew little of Frank's past and perhaps it was better that way. It was only in the last few months, with the imminent arrival of his first child, that Fin had discovered Frank was actually married. He knew he was lucky being partnered with Frank. Originally, he'd been allocated to Bérnard.

"Anyone got a flash-bang?" asked Frank, breaking the silence.

"What d'you want one of those for?" asked Bérnard.

"Yeah, I got one," answered McCoote, ignoring his partner's comment.

"Okay," continued Frank. "I'm going to rig that door…"

"Who put you in charge Reynolds?" interrupted Bérnard.

"Listen, if SWAT have gone in the front, which way do you think the bad guys are going to be heading?"

"Errr…"

"We put a flash-bang across that door and well, it should give us some warning at least."

"Sure Frank," said Fin. "That way we'll be ready when they come."

Neither Bérnard nor McCoote had anything to add and so, using the access card he'd been given earlier, Frank quickly opened the door and disappeared inside.

"He forgot the flash-bang" said McCoote a few seconds later.

What the hell are you doing Frank? This isn't your problem.

Frank tried to ignore this question and others as he hurried down the darkened passageway. He knew SWAT were here because some fool was worried about career damage and sending them in early like this probably meant the hostages were as good as dead. That was not something he could just ignore.

Finding a stairwell at the end of the corridor, Frank hurried upwards until he saw a sign saying Basement Level Four. He knew the hostages were being kept somewhere on this level, but how to reach them? He had few options, but after a quick search, Frank found what he was looking for. The building had ventilation shafts running throughout it and all of them were fitted with inspection panels. Balancing on the staircase railings, Frank managed to remove one of the panels before gently easing himself upwards and into the nearest shaft. It was cramped inside, but just about wide enough for him to crawl along. Frank paused to listen. So far he'd heard nothing but silence, but was that a good thing? *Maybe the terrorists were preoccupied with SWAT? What if the hostages had been left alone?* Frank berated himself. It was no good second guessing what he didn't know. *One step at a time*, he thought, repeating the old mantra of Delta Force before starting to move forwards to find out.

Very slowly, Frank slid his body the last few inches along the ventilation shaft. He'd been listening to the soft cries and whisperings of the hostages for a while now and knew if he made even the slightest of noises, it might be his undoing. Sound travelled easily along these thin metal tubes. Finally, after what seemed like hours, he reached the grill at the end and stretched forward to look out. His elevated position gave him almost full sight of the room and he immediately spotted the hostages. Six teenage girls sat huddled in one corner, all of them looking terrified. As to which one was the governor's daughter, Frank didn't know or for that matter really care. They were all in trouble.

For the next five minutes, Frank forced himself to do nothing but watch. It took a lot of patience not to act immediately, but that was the secret of reconnaissance. *Use what you observe to your advantage*, was another important doctrine he'd learnt at Delta. For a start, Frank knew the girls were alone and from their whispered conversations, he now knew the guard had left fifteen minutes ago. The terrorist had received a radio call, one in a language the girls didn't understand, then hurried off leaving them alone in the room. He'd stopped briefly to lock the door behind him. Although Frank couldn't see it, he guessed from the girls' anxious looks that the door was somewhere below where he was now. The only other objects in the room were some stacks of chairs and a solitary table. He didn't have much to work with, but a plan was starting to form...

BOOM!

Another explosion echoed throughout the building and Frank's mind was made up for him. He slammed his palm against the grill and, after another four or five blows, he managed to knock it out. The grill went flying across the room and he quickly shuffled forwards to see the girls staring at him in terror and confusion. Frank put a finger to his lips before pointing to the CPD badge on his arm. He saw hope in their eyes and when he pointed to the table, they immediately seemed to understand his plan. Two of them got to their feet and started to move towards it, but when the door opened, everyone froze. One of the terrorists walked into the room and instantly sensed that something was wrong. Frank's head was sticking out of the shaft only feet above him. He knew he only had one chance. He had to get the gun out of his leg holster without being heard.

"Sit down," said the guard in a thick accent, waving the two girls back to the others with his rifle. "Don't move."

Slowly, Frank started to move his right hand down his leg and he'd got as far as touching the gun when the terrorist turned around.

The look of surprise on the guard's face quickly turned to hatred and Frank knew he was about to die. As the guard raised his rifle, Frank spotted movement. "You don't have to do this…" he began, stalling for time.

The guard smiled as he slowly took aim. When the metal grill smashed him across the head, he dropped like a stone. Ignoring the height drop, Frank slid out of the shaft and went crashing to the floor. He felt ribs snap, but, fighting the pain, quickly got up and had his weapon to hand in seconds. Frank kicked at the guard, but the grill had done its job, the terrorist was out cold.

"Well done," he said to the girl.

She smiled and began to speak, but Frank interrupted her.

"Listen up. We don't have much time and I need you to act quickly. Here, help me move that table."

Between them, they carried the table across the small room and placed it directly under the shaft.

"Once you're in there, keep going to the end and then turn right. Eventually you'll come across a hole by some stairs. Get out of the shaft, take the stairs to the bottom floor and follow the corridor. There should be a door at the end and outside are three policemen. You got that?" The girls all nodded. "Okay, I'll stay here until you're clear. Now move!"

Realising they might live through this after all, the six girls needed no further encouragement and, within minutes, the last of them was crawling down the shaft to freedom. Checking the guard was still out cold, Frank quickly holstered his own gun and with a series of swift, practiced moves, he removed the firing mechanism from the guard's rifle. Minutes later and he was in the shaft himself. Only then did he breathe a bit more easily.

Frank went through the door with his arms held high. An amplified voice ordered him to his knees and he obeyed immediately.

"It's okay, it's Frank. Lower your weapons," ordered the Chief of Police as he walked over and helped Frank to his feet.

"Thanks Chief," said Frank, wincing slightly at the pain in his ribs. "They all get out okay?"

The older man nodded. "All accounted for."

"Bad guys?"

"Without the hostages they had nothing. SWAT have neutralised the threat."

"That's good. You seen Fin?"

"He's out front helping with the hostages. If you ask me, I'd say he's trying to get a date."

Frank laughed, trying to picture his partner mixing with the daughters of the Chicago elite.

"That wasn't the cleverest thing to do Frank," said the chief, his face turning serious. "Brave, yes, but not very clever."

"Yeah, you can put that on my tombstone," replied Frank with a grin as he walked off to find his partner.

He'd just left the alleyway when a girl's voice called out to him.

"Hey officer… officer, wait up!"

Frank turned to see a blonde girl hurrying towards him. He recognized her as the one who'd floored the guard with the metal grill.

"Hey, I just wanted to say thanks," she said. "You know, thanks for what you did."

"No problem," replied Frank. "You did pretty well in there yourself."

"I don't know what came over me. What if I'd missed him or something? What if it had all gone wrong?"

"But it didn't. Sometimes you have to make a choice. This time you got it right; maybe next time you won't be so lucky."

"Sounds like experience."

"Yeah, too much experience," said Frank softly as he turned to go.

"Hey officer, what's your name?"

"Frank," he replied without looking back.

"Frank what?"

"Just Frank."

"Well okay, Officer Just Frank," she continued, still talking to his back. "My name's Helena… Helena Larrouy. If you ever need my family's help or anything, just let me know. Okay?"

Frank didn't reply. He doubted he'd ever need the help of a family like Johan Larrouy's.

CHAPTER SIX

The plane touched down with a bump, shaking Frank from his thoughts and causing him to smile. After months of hiding away in his apartment, making little headway into finding those responsible for murdering his family, it felt good to be actually doing something about it for a change.

But as he stepped out of the private jet, Frank immediately wished he'd packed more clothing. Despite the fact his metallic limbs could simulate the cold, the rest of his body was suddenly subjected to the icy Russian air and it wasn't pleasant. Dr Brown had already left the jet and was standing at the base of its steps in conversation with a group of people obviously awaiting their arrival.

As Frank descended the steps himself, he watched a small man in black fatigues approach. The man had emerged from an old-fashioned, gas-engined car parked between two blacked-out Humvees and was obviously here for him.

"COLT-45, I'm Swamps," said the man with an outstretched hand.

"Actually," replied Frank, taking his hand, "my name's Frank."

The man simply smiled. Frank had spent enough time in Special Forces to recognise one of his own. Many soldiers with that kind of specialist training found themselves later working in the private security sector, often doing questionable things for questionable people.

"Okay, let's go," said Swamps, turning towards the car and presumably expecting Frank to follow. "The meeting's in an hour and we've gotta fit your interface."

"Interface?"

"This," replied the man with a grin, holding up what appeared to be a metallic finger, one almost identical to Frank's own. "We'll swap it for one of yours. The connection you'll need for the mainframe's hidden inside, along with a communicator. Pretty neat, eh?"

"We're going to attach it in the car?"

"You see any hospitals around here?" grinned the smaller man. "Anyway, the car journey's too short, so we'll have to do it in the chopper. But don't worry, it won't hurt too much."

Frank decided he really didn't like this guy at all. By now, several other men, also dressed in combat fatigues, had emerged from the waiting Humvees and were collecting the bags. They too, all looked quietly competent and, if Frank guessed correctly, were just as deadly as their leader.

"So, you guys are my back up?"

Swamps stopped by the car and turned to face

Frank. "We're here to see nothing happens to her," he replied, nodding towards Helena. "No one mentioned anything about you."

<><><>

The thumping of the Chinook's rotor blades increased in volume as the helicopter slowly approached the landing site, which, according to Swamps, was only a few hundred metres from their destination. The team leader was now acting as the aircraft's loadmaster and, during the short flight, Frank had watched as the rest of his team were carefully hidden beneath the false flooring. Clearly Larrouy was taking no chances with his granddaughter, but at the same time, he obviously didn't want to raise any suspicions.

The chopper touched down and Swamps grinned as Frank walked down the rear ramp, following on after Helena and her aides.

"Have fun," he shouted after them. Frank remained calm, somehow resisting the urge to morph a blade and ram it through the smaller man's neck. Emerging from the helicopter and into the cold air, which was somewhat at odds with the bright sunlight, Frank followed the others along a path leading from the helipad towards a rather nondescript-looking building. Unlike the flamboyant, high-rise skyscrapers of corporate America, the headquarters of CCR were obviously built out of necessity. Compact and only two storeys high, the structure was designed to withstand the cold, Russian weather rather than advertise the success of its wealthy owners.

The small party stopped at the main security gate,

where an officious looking man in a smart suit began talking to Helena. Two large security guards checked for identification before starting to conduct electronic scans of the group as they all waited in turn to pass through the gate. Frank couldn't help but note the impressive security measures. Electrically-charged fencing ran in double layers around the site and he'd already spotted multiple camera arrays, each one covering every possible angle. This place was clearly serious about security, but just how serious remained to be seen. He glanced down at his right hand, looking for any evidence of where the 'interface' finger had been attached. The truth was it looked no different to before, but would it be enough to fool the scanners? Keeping in mind just how important the information on TALIR could be, Frank had to take the chance.

"So, you're the interpreter?" asked the guard in perfect English.

"Afraid so," replied Frank with a small smile. "Told them I wouldn't be needed, but she's the boss."

The guard grinned back.

"We have a strange dialect around these parts," began the guard, now speaking in local Siberian. "Most Russians wouldn't understand what I'm saying, let alone some American fool."

"Good job this American fool didn't translate any of that then," replied Frank with a grin, pleased to see surprise register on the guard's face. During the exchange, the other guard had started to scan Frank's body with a complex -looking detector.

"That's a lot of robotics," he stated simply after finishing his sweep.

"Landmine," replied Frank coolly.

The guard nodded and asked no further questions. No matter what side of a war you'd fought on, ex-soldiers were respectful of one another's past.

"Everything check out?" asked the Russian official and, after receiving a nod from the guards, he turned to go. "Follow me please. We're to go directly to the Meeting Room."

Frank breathed a small sigh of relief. *So far so good*, he thought nervously. *But now comes the hard part.*

Above the building's main entrance, Frank spotted a small sign that read 'Cyber Corps Russia.' Apart from that, there was little else to show this as the headquarters of one of the biggest robotics companies in the world. *Must be offices*, he reasoned, *it's surely not big enough for any production floors too.*

Once inside, they were led down several empty corridors before going up a flight of stairs. A short walk along another corridor and they stopped before a set of unmarked doors. Frank had only spotted a couple of other people within the building and most of the doors they passed were closed. It was strangely unnerving.

"Please go in," said their guide with a forced smile as he opened the door for them.

Helena led the way and, as soon as they entered, three smartly-dressed men stood up from behind a large, mahogany table.

"Dr Brown," began the tallest of the men. "Thank you for coming at such short notice."

"It's my pleasure Mr Redski," replied Helena, addressing the man she knew was the senior of the three directors before her. "Hopefully we can move forward with those proposals now I'm here in person."

"Please, take a seat," said another of the Russian men. "I believe you're happy with the agenda?"

"Of course," replied Helena with a smile and, as soon as they were all sitting down, the discussions began in earnest. Frank quickly found he wasn't needed for translation as the Russians spoke fluent English, and so he resigned himself to simply waiting. Most of the discussions went over his head; a lot of it being complicated technical talk or financial offers. Instead, he found himself staring impassively at the three Russians before him. Could these men really be the ones bankrolling TALIR? Were they truly responsible for murdering his family? It was hard not to let his feelings show. *Remember,* he told himself, *you're here for answers. Stick to the plan and you'll get them.* Frank knew he'd only have one chance to get this right and so, after about an hour of having his patience severely tested, he decided that chance was now.

"Sorry," he began, interrupting the discussions. "But where are the restrooms?" One of the Russians looked across at him, a flicker of annoyance showing in his eyes.

"Outside, turn left and straight to the end of the corridor," he replied briskly.

To her credit, Helena didn't so much as glance at Frank as he spoke, despite her knowledge of the dangerous sequence of events that were about to be set in motion.

Frank quietly excused himself and left the room unnoticed. Once outside, he checked the corridor was clear and then, as he'd been shown by Swamps, released a small catch on his interface finger. The tip immediately came loose and slowly motored outwards. With his free hand, he carefully removed the end and pushed it into his ear. A small click indicated the microphone was live.

"Larrouy?" he asked in a whisper.

"Here," came the reply into his earpiece. "Okay, I've got your position. Turn right, right again and look for the elevators."

Knowing time was against them, Frank quickly found the elevators and then pressed the call button, the right-hand set of doors opening immediately.

"Fifth floor down," said the voice in his ear as he entered the elevator. He looked at the buttons before him and pressed number five. *This thing goes to basement level twenty*, he though with surprise. *What the hell is this place?* Frank was still considering this when the elevator suddenly stopped only one floor down. The doors slid open and an elderly, academic-looking man wearing a white over-suit walked in. Frank desperately tried to ignore him and look natural.

"I've not seen you here before," began the man as the elevator started moving again. "Are you new?"

"Err… yes… just transferred in," replied Frank in perfect Russian, but having to think on his feet.

"That's funny… I've not been notified of any new personnel," said the man, narrowing his eyes and staring hard at Frank over the top of his old style, wire-rimmed glasses.

"It was a last minute thing," replied Frank with a half-hearted laugh. "You know how this place is."

He leaned closer to Frank. "Who are you? What's your clearance number?"

"Err, I haven't got one of those yet." answered Frank.

"I'm calling security," said the older man, removing a communicator from his inside pocket.

"Deal with it," ordered a voice in his ear.

Frank put a metal hand on the man's arm to stop him raising the communicator.

"What...?"

His other suddenly whipped upwards in a crunching blow to the man's chin, causing him to drop like a stone. As Frank lowered the body to the floor, Larrouy's voice broke through again.

"Leave him there; you're approaching the fifth floor." The elevator slowed to a halt and its doors drew open. Thankfully, the corridor was empty. "The door at the end, entry code 3641... the mainframe's in there."

Frank dashed up to the door and, after punching in the access code, watched it swing open. Entering the heavily air-conditioned room, he paused in awe at the sight before him. Rack upon rack of supercomputers completely filled the large room, each one stretching off into the gloomy distance.

"Find the row labelled Alpha Bravo Three Delta. It's about half way down your left side."

Frank set off in that direction, checking the numbers on each row as he went. "Got it," he answered after a short time.

"Okay, activate the interface like you were shown and put it into the socket marked 'DTS Output'."

Frank spotted the socket immediately. He then touched another small button on his finger and a thin, golden plug appeared from out of the missing tip. Without waiting for any further instructions, he pushed it into the socket. Strangely, Frank felt nothing at all, and as time ticked slowly by, he could only hope the data was being transferred.

"Now what?"

"When it flashes, take it out," came the reply.

Frank felt strangely redundant as he stood there waiting for something to happen. Suddenly, the interface started flashing with a green glow. "Okay, it's flashing."

"Take it out and get back to that room before you're missed. And remember the earpiece."

Frank needed no further encouragement. He quickly retracted the interface and put the earpiece back in place. Then, spinning around, he raced back towards the door. Feeling like he might pull this off after all, he swung open the door to face an equally surprised looking security guard.

"Who are you? What are you doing in there?"

"Sorry," began Frank, recovering quickly. "I'm looking for the restroom."

"This is a restricted area."

"I must have taken a wrong turn."

"Are you with the Americans?"

Frank was torn. Should he neutralise the guard like he had the man in the elevator... *The man in the elevator!* thought Frank frantically. *Had the guard seen him? No, he'd have his weapon out. Dammit, things were starting to go downhill fast.*

"Okay," said Frank with a forced smile. "Why don't we just go back to the meeting room? I'm sure we can sort things out there?" The guard looked at him suspiciously before nodding for Frank to lead off. As they approached the elevators, Frank made a decision. If the left-hand set of doors opened to reveal the body, he'd quickly have to take the guard out. Tensing himself for action, he pressed the call button. When the right-hand doors slid open, he gave a small prayer of thanks. He had a few minutes more to think of a way out of this mess.

CHAPTER SEVEN

"I think you've got some explaining to do, Dr Brown," said Mr Redski. Frank had been escorted back to the meeting room by the guard, who remained close by his side as he apologised for getting lost.

"Explain how? He got lost, end of story," replied Helena, wondering if she sounded as nervous as she felt. "Look, we've made good progress today; let's not spoil that shall we?"

"Doctor, please don't take me for a fool. A simple trip to the restroom ends up at our mainframe?" Redski leant forward on the table. "You might want to think very carefully about what you say next."

"Are you threatening me?" answered Helena calmly.

"Not at all Dr Brown. But tell me, how well do you know this man Reynolds? What if he's working for someone else? Someone willing to pay…"

"Just what exactly are you accusing him of?"

interrupted Helena angrily.

The Russian continued to smile back at her. "We're about to find out."

"How?" asked Helena. "You've already scanned him twice and found nothing. Why? Because there's nothing to find! It's like he said, he got lost!"

"Dr Brown, as we speak, I've got technicians running several highly-sophisticated inspection programs through our servers. Very soon we'll know if Mr Reynolds even breathed on the mainframe."

Frank tried to remain calm. This was the moment he'd feared might come, the moment Helena would be left with no choice. The reputation of Cyber-Tech was on the line, as was her career. Surely she must do as her grandfather ordered? Frank looked into her eyes to see her staring back at him with equal intensity. She'd supported his story so far, but when the technicians discovered he'd accessed the mainframe…

"Frank…" she whispered, lowering her eyes.

Frank felt numb. Somehow, he'd always thought…

"Deal with the guard," she said suddenly.

Frank was so sure he'd heard her wrong, that for a moment he remained frozen in place. Then, before anyone else could act, he brought a metallic elbow crashing upwards into the guard's nose and leapt forward. Sliding across the wooden table, he landed between the shocked-looking Russians and, before the unconscious guard had even hit the floor, Frank had a blade against Redski's throat. He had to grit his teeth against the pain of the morph. He knew if he succumbed to its side effects now, everything was over.

"Americans. You simply can't be trusted," said Redski calmly. The other directors were now on their feet protesting.

"Sit down, all of you," demanded Helena, "and pass me your phones."

"Dr Brown…" began one of her visibly shocked aides, "shouldn't we at least…"

"Get your stuff together, we're leaving," she interrupted, turning back towards the Russian men and quickly collecting their phones.

"You won't get away with this," said Redski.

"Watch us," replied Frank, leaning in towards the Russian with a smile.

"Dr Brown," he continued, ignoring Frank completely, "escape from this building is impossible. Whatever you've stolen, surely it's not worth your lives?"

"Frank..." began Helena, her eyes betraying how nervous she felt, "it's your choice."

She left the rest of the question unsaid, but Frank realized what she was asking. As his mind raced, he knew deep down that he couldn't just kill these men in cold blood. Without seeing any evidence linking them to TALIR, they were innocent. He slowly shook his head and saw relief etched in Helena's eyes as well as those of the Russians. For all his earlier bravado, Redski briefly looked like a man who'd just realized how close to death he'd been. Slowly removing the blade from Redski's throat, Frank watched as Helena and her aides left the room.

"I know about TALIR," he whispered in the Russian's ear.

No reply.

"And if I find out you're responsible…"

Suddenly alarm bells began to sound throughout the building.

"Dammit," said Frank and, with another curse, he turned and hurried for the door, leaving the three Russians smiling in his wake.

"Which way?" shouted Helena as he caught up with them a little way down the corridor.

"Down the stairs and then…"

"Stop!" came a sudden order from behind. Ignoring the shout, the small group reached the top of the stairs and hurried on downwards. Bringing up the rear, Frank had only just cleared the corridor when the first shots rang out.

"Run!" he shouted, ushering them downwards faster. Bullets ricocheted off the wall behind them and it was at that point Frank realize realized they probably wouldn't make it out of there alive. He'd always planned to fight his way out if necessary, but not like this. Of all the scenarios he'd envisioned, bringing Helena and her aides with him hadn't been one of them.

What the hell am I supposed to do now? Frank asked himself. *Abandon them?* In all of his military years, Frank had never left a man behind and he wasn't about to start now.

"Turn right!" he ordered as they reached the ground floor. "Let me go first in case of…"

BOOM!

Everyone stumbled as a huge blast tore down the corridor. Frank helped Helena to her feet and had to shout to make himself heard over the noise of several other smaller explosions.

"Down the corridor… MOVE!"

That first explosion came from outside, he thought with renewed hope. Suddenly more gunshots rang out, this time ahead of them.

"Keep going! Run!" he repeated, grabbing hold of Helena's arm and helping her along. She was clearly terrified and Frank knew he had to do his best to reassure her.

"Don't worry," he shouted over the racket of further explosions and gunfire. "I'm pretty sure all that noise means help's on the way."

As if on cue, Swamps sprinted around the corner and skidded to a halt. The small man kept his weapon trained on Frank for longer than was necessary, before, with a grin, lowering it slowly towards the floor.

"Knew this plan wouldn't work," he said, still grinning at Frank. "You'd better follow me," and with that, he turned and started running back the way he'd just come. Swamps led them at pace down the smoke-filled corridor, heading roughly towards where Frank guessed the main entrance would be.

Suddenly gunfire echoed around them and shrapnel started to fly in all directions. One of Dr Brown's aides cried out in pain.

"Everyone down!" shouted Swamps, kneeling to return fire. Finding whatever cover they could, the small group dropped to the floor as Frank strained to see through the smoke. *That gunfire had come from ahead. Was the way out blocked? Jesus,* thought Frank, *Unless Swamps can get some more of his men into the building, we're trapped.*

"Where's the rest of your men?" he shouted to over the clamour of more detonations.

"Not stupid enough to follow I guess," came the

reply.

Great, thought Frank, *we're trapped in a secure building, surrounded by well-armed Russian guards and our only hope of escape rests with this psychotic idiot. Guess it's up to me to sort this mess out after all.*

"Everyone get ready to move out!" shouted Frank to the group. Pointing his arm towards the wall opposite, he sent the necessary signal to his Cortex and said a quick prayer. The morphing took less than a second, his metallic arm quickly shaping, growing and developing into exactly the weapon Frank had asked for... a short-range cannon.

"Take cover!" he called and, with another command to his Cortex, he fired several explosive charges at the wall. *Not an ideal plan,* thought Frank, *but we're running out of options here.* A series of short, percussive blasts blew the corridor wall apart, showering them all in dust and debris. Frank heard several more cries of pain, but as the dust began to settle, he saw to his relief that his somewhat desperate plan had worked. A ragged hole had appeared in the corridor wall and through it, Frank could see daylight.

"Quickly, everyone out!" he shouted, grateful to see the entire group getting to their feet. No one needed to be told twice and with Swamps giving covering fire, they clambered out through the hole.

As he'd hoped, Swamps' team were waiting outside. The heavily armed men were crouched near to where a large portion of the perimeter fence was now missing; its bent and twisted remains clear evidence of one of the earlier explosions. The black-clothed soldiers hurried forward to meet them and, before long, the sorry looking group were racing back towards the waiting helicopter.

More bullets began to crack through the air and, turning, Frank saw to his dismay that the guard force had regrouped.

"Okay, fire the Wall," Swamps ordered, speaking into his communicator as he ran.

WHOOMPH!

Frank felt a pressure wave from behind, quickly followed by intense heat. Turning as he ran, he saw a six foot wall of flame now blocking any pursuit. It spread for hundreds of meters in both directions, forming an impenetrable barrier and Frank had to smile. Swamps had set off an Incendiary Wall and that, he knew, was some high-tech ordnance. From his time in Delta, he remembered how a 'Wall' was transported as a lightweight roll of flammable composites and, once rolled out in a line, could be used to aid any escape. Fired by remote signal, the wall of flames was designed to last long enough to give a team of soldiers the chance of orderly retreat. Manufactured and sold by Cyber-Tech, Frank couldn't help but smile at the irony.

"That fire won't last all day," shouted Swamps to the group. "Keep running for the chopper!"

The group needed no further encouragement and for the first time Frank thought they might actually make it. He turned towards Helena and saw a similar look in her own eyes.

"That was all a bit close…" he began.

"Roger… understood. We're cleared for phase two," shouted Swamps, talking into another radio he'd just been handed by one of his men.

Frank stopped what he was about to say to Helena. Suddenly, this seemed a lot more important. "Phase two? What the hell's phase two?"

Swamps didn't answer. Instead, he carried on listening to the radio's earpiece as they hurried towards the helicopter.

"Affirmative, we're all ready here, sir," said the team leader, continuing to ignore Frank.

Suddenly Frank saw Helena's eyes go wide.

"Oh God, no…" she whispered before making a sudden grab for the radio in Swamps' hand. Catching him unprepared, she tore it out of his grasp and immediately stopped running. Frank and Swamps were the only ones to stop with her.

"That wall ain't gonna last much longer," began Swamps. "You might wanna reconsider… well, whatever the hell it is you're doing."

Helena ignored him and continued pressing buttons on the radio, trying to talk into it at the same time.

"Stop this," she demanded angrily, looking the sneering team leader in the eyes. "Call it off."

"Sorry ma'am," he replied, still with something of a grin. "Mr Larrouy's orders."

"Then let me speak to him," she snapped, once again attempting to get the radio to work.

"You can't, the sat-link's been cut."

Helena turned away from him and quickly pulled out her cell phone.

"What's going on? Are you calling Larrouy?" asked Frank with growing concern.

"No goddamn signal!" she said, staring angrily at the phone in her hand.

"Helena, what…" began Frank, but before he'd even had time to finish his question, she was sprinting off back towards the fire wall.

"HEY! HEY, YOU OVER THERE!" she

screamed.

"Jesus, what's she doing?" asked Frank.

Swamps remained standing where he was. "You wanna get her, or shall I?" he asked with a grin.

One day, I'm going to wipe that grin off your face with my fist, thought Frank as he raced off after her.

Helena was stood before the dying flame wall as he approached, waving her arms and shouting something about an evacuation. Frank could just make out the guards through the receding flames. They seemed a bit unsure whether to open fire or not, and it was at that moment he saw it.

Just a speck in the sky at first, but rapidly growing in size as it streaked towards them.

"Oh Christ…" was all he managed, before a blinding flash, quickly followed by a shockwave of energy, blew him off his feet. When the noise arrived, it was deafening. Frank curled up into a ball and stayed there until he'd both heard and felt the debris around him stop falling. Slowly sitting up, he shook his head to clear it and as he did so, he spotted Helena. She was lying on the ground a short distance away and wasn't moving. In the distance, behind him, nothing now remained of the building they'd been in minutes only before. The structure was completely gone. Its outer walls were blown to pieces and huge chunks of concrete, some of which lay only a few yards away, covered the area all around. Where the centre of building had once been, a fire burned with desperate ferocity and from what remained of the guards, Frank knew it was nothing short of a miracle he'd survived.

He'd only briefly seen the missile before it hit and now, witnessing its terrible aftermath, he guessed it was a 'Double B'. The 'Bunker Buster' was designed to penetrate deeply and cause maximum sub-surface damage. Frank knew there'd be little chance of any survivors; he'd seen the results of precision ordnance like this before. Shaking himself from the memories, Frank clambered to his feet. Praying that Helena was okay, he moved towards her and, to his relief, saw she was beginning to stir.

"Helena. Helena, you okay?"

"Yes, yes, I'm fine, I think," she replied a little unsteadily as Frank helped her to sit upright. At that point Swamps arrived, looking around as if nothing unusual had happened.

"Okay people, we really gotta go."

"Just like that?" replied Frank furiously as he got Helena back to her feet. "Don't you realize what you've just done? Yes, yes, of course you do. This was the plan all along, wasn't it?" Frank turned to look at Helena, his eyes hard with anger. "Did you know about the missile too?"

"No, of course not Frank," replied Helena groggily. "After I heard that radio call about phase two, well…"

"Yes, you tried to stop it," said Frank, feeling some of his anger towards her draining away.

"Too little, too late," she said with a sigh, looking towards what remained of the ruined building. "I guess stealing the data was only part of his plan. The directors of CCR, all together in one place and…"

"It's time to get rid of the competition," Frank finished as he turned to face Swamps. Moving slowly towards the team leader, he raised a fist and morphed it into a glistening blade. Frank was pleased to see the man's trademark smirk slip a bit. Out of the corner of his eye, he was aware of Swamp's men arriving and then gradually beginning to spread out around him.

"Stand down COLT-45," ordered Swamps, ignoring the deadly weapon now held only inches from his face.

"I've told you before, my name's Frank you piece of sh…"

"Let's just cool things shall we?" interrupted Helena, standing between them. As she spoke, she saw a hardness in Frank's eyes she'd not seen before and realized she was looking at a different man. A man who'd killed numerous times for his country… and a man just about to take on an entire team of Spec Ops soldiers.

"I said to stand down," repeated Swamps, the rest of his team now raising their weapons towards Frank. "You're outnumbered and outgunned."

"Frank, it's okay. Look, we can sort this out," began Helena softly. "We can…"

"No," snapped Frank. "No, it's not okay." Leaning towards Swamps he spoke very calmly. "I might be outnumbered, but as for outgunned."

Although he'd been experimenting with more complicated morphs for months, Frank knew he was about to enter new territory. This would take everything he had. The change started slowly at first, but then, as he asked the Cortex for more, it began to accelerate.

"Arrgghh," he cried, feeling the strain within his head as the Morphing Cortex reacted to the massive demands he was asking of it.

In his anger, Frank had decided to gamble and, thankfully for him, it seemed to have paid off.

Helena stood staring at him, mouth open in

amazement. Even Swamps looked uncertain what to do, his men looking blankly for orders.

Adjusting his balance to the change in weight, Frank swung his massive arms to point towards them and smiled as they all flinched back. Understandable perhaps, as they were now staring into the barrels of two highly developed, multi-functional, tetra-jet ion cannons, both of which now hummed with barely constrained power. Frank even managed a smile before his Cortex overloaded and everything went black.

Helena knelt over Frank's body, her face awash with concern. He was still unresponsive; both eyes had rolled fully backwards and his mouth hung open, drooling freely.

"It's okay Frank," she whispered to him. "I'll help you through this." One of Swamps' men came running back from the helicopter with the medical bag she'd asked for. Removing a large electro-syringe, Helena placed it against Frank's neck and slowly pressed the release button. "Okay, he's asleep," she said, turning towards the team leader. "Help me get him on board."

"My orders didn't cover…" began Swamps.

"Well they do now," she snapped back. Despite the huge weaponry on his arms, Helena somehow managed to get the unconscious Frank into a sitting position.

"I'll need confirmation," Swamps insisted, still watching her struggle.

"You'll get your goddamn confirmation," she shouted angrily. "Now please, just help me."

Eventually Swamps nodded and ordered his men

to help lift Frank into the waiting helicopter. As he was being carried away, Helena looked from Frank towards the still burning compound and realized a simple truth. In the space of a few short hours, everything about her life had suddenly been turned upside down.

CHAPTER EIGHT

"Stealing the data wasn't enough for you, was it?" asked Helena angrily. She'd tried to remain calm in front of her grandfather, but it hadn't lasted very long. "No, you had to go further still; you had to remove the competition. Corporate espionage is one thing, but this was murder."

"Yes, very regrettable," answered Larrouy, sitting behind his huge, wooden desk and looking completely unaffected by his granddaughter's outburst. His office sat at the top of the giant Cyber-Tech building and it had a 360 degree view of the city. 'His' city was how he liked to think of it.

"Regrettable?" she asked, stunned at his choice of words.

"Perhaps, but look at our gains. Cyber Corp Russia is finished as a company. Its shares have crashed, its factories are closed and no one wants to take control."

"Thanks to you and your missiles."

Larrouy smiled. "That can't be proved."

Helena sighed; she had known it was going to be a pointless discussion from the start. She'd been so busy helping Frank recover from his ordeal that it had taken her a week to even come up here. Granted she'd put it off for her own reasons too, but when it came down to it, she'd known she'd have to face her grandfather sometime.

"So, when do you want to restart COLT?" asked Larrouy.

"You just don't get it, do you?" replied Helena. "There is no COLT. The project's dead, it's a failure."

"Not true. Frank Reynolds is proof of that."

Helena sighed. "When Frank's well again, I'm letting him go, and you'd better not try and stop me."

"Yes, I thought you'd say that. But why not start again without him? I'll find you some new subjects; ones perhaps less troublesome."

"I'm sorry, but no" Helena replied. She knew what she was about to give up, but was determined to go through with it all the same. "What you did was wrong and the worst part is, you can't even see it. I'm through with Cyber-Tech."

"Don't be rash Helena."

"I'm not being rash, I'm simply being honest," she replied and, with that, Helena turned towards the door.

"You'll be back," her grandfather called after her with a knowing smile.

Helena held her tongue and left the room without another word.

Yes, thought Johan Larrouy, still smiling, *you'll be back. For a start, you're not a bit like your mother.*

Suddenly the intercom on his desk buzzed,

interrupting his thoughts.

"What is it?" asked Larrouy, his smile fading.

"Dr Crawford's here to see you, sir."

"Send him in."

The man who entered the room was tall, gaunt and, although in his mid-thirties, he looked older. Dr Crawford was a brilliant scientist, but Larrouy knew he'd always resented working under Helena and so when one door closed...

"Dr Crawford," he began. "I'm a busy man, so I'll come straight to the point. I'm looking to restart the COLT project. Would you be interested?"

The tall doctor looked taken aback. "Restart the COLT Project? But sir, surely Dr Brown..."

"... is no longer in the picture," Larrouy finished for him.

Crawford smiled, not something he did very often. "Well in that case..."

"Good, then it's decided," interrupted Larrouy. "You can start by analysing the Russian data."

"But hasn't that already been done, sir? The files were unreadable, corrupted after COLT-45 overloaded his Cortex. Perhaps..."

"A decoy," broke in Larrouy.

"Errr... sorry, a what?"

"The real data was removed from COLT-45's Cortex before he ever returned to Cyber-Tech. It was replaced with a decoy."

Larrouy could tell by the look on Crawford's face that he wasn't interested in politics and scheming, he just wanted to know what the true data might reveal. Larrouy couldn't have planned it better. "This," he continued, holding up small memory stick, "is everything we got from the CCR mainframe."

Crawford took the stick from Larrouy's outstretched hand. He could hardly contain his excitement and was now smiling like a kid at Christmas.

"No one outside of COLT is to know about this," said Larrouy.

"Yes…yes of course, sir. I fully understand."

When Dr Crawford left his office a short time later, Larrouy couldn't help but gloat. Everything was going according to plan.

Suddenly, the intercom sounded.

"Yes?"

"Sir, the footage you asked for, it's ready,"

"Thank you, Mary. Send it through."

"Streaming now, sir."

As Larrouy watched the screen in front of him, his smile widened. Reaching forward, he picked up the secure phone.

"Mary, ask the Chief of Defense to see me at his earliest convenience."

"Yes, of course, sir"

"Oh, and Mary."

"Sir?"

"I'll expect him within the hour."

When Frank awoke, he found himself back in his old room at Cyber-Tech. As memories of Russia rushed back to him, so did his anger. He leapt from his bed, heedless of the wires and monitors attached to his body and immediately attempted another big morph. Unfortunately for Frank, COLT had anticipated this reaction and taken measures to prevent it. Two small tranq-darts hit him in the chest before his weapons were even half-formed and within seconds he was asleep.

Through the one-way glass, Helena watched as Frank was lifted back onto his bed by several orderlies, the weight of his semi-morphed arms causing them to struggle.

"Call me when he wakes," she ordered before turning to leave. Helena could afford to wait a bit longer and besides, she had an office to clear.

<><><>

Frank sat on the edge of his bed experimenting with different morphs. Nothing too big, he didn't want to upset any trigger-happy scientists again, but enough to keep him occupied. Memories of Russia whirled around in his head, making him want to lash out in anger and so he channeled his energies into morphing instead. Frank wanted answers, but he also knew the only way to get them was to play by Cyber-Tech's rules. He hated being cornered like this, but perhaps there was still some hope left, and she was due here any minute.

"How are you feeling Frank?" asked Helena, walking into the room.

For some reason, one Frank couldn't quite put his finger on yet, he thought she looked different. Her face was drawn with fatigue, but there was something else, something different about her demeanour.

"I'm fine thanks, doctor. By the way, am I your prisoner again?"

"No," she replied immediately, taking Frank by surprise.

"What do you mean?"

"We're not keeping you here Frank," she replied, moving to sit next to him on the bed, "and I've removed your last tracker."

"Damn, I thought I'd got them all. Where'd you hide it?"

"It was actually part of the Cortex; you'd never have found it yourself," replied Helena.

"So that's how you got me downtown."

"We never really lost you, Frank."

"So I'm free to go and no one's going to stop me, not even your grandfather?"

"No," she replied simply.

Frank stood up, ready to leave, but with a sigh, he slowly sat back down again. There were just too many unanswered questions.

"Look, before I go, I reckon you owe me some answers, Helena."

She didn't reply and Frank began to think she never would. Then, in a soft voice, she started to speak.

"What do you want to know Frank?"

"The data we stole from Russia. Tell me you found something to justify wiping out CCR."

"Sorry Frank, but we got nothing. The data was corrupt, totally unreadable."

"But how?" asked Frank, barely able to hide his disappointment.

"We think that when you morphed, it somehow overloaded the Cortex and the data got fried."

"Jesus," sighed Frank. "There's nothing? You tried everything?"

"You've been in a coma for a week Frank. I've spent that whole time trying to find something, anything, to defend what we did."

"What *we* did?" said Frank, feeling his anger rise again. "Don't put any of this on me Helena; this was your grandfather's plan from the start. He's the only one around here happy the way things have turned out. Business rivals gone, TALIR now leaderless, hell, even COLT's a reality. Restart the project and he's got his own army." Frank stood up and turned to face her. "So tell me Helena, when do you start work on COLT-46?"

"I'm not going back to COLT, Frank."

"But why? Your project's a success, you've got…"

"I've resigned," she answered.

Frank stared at her in surprise.

"I'm done with COLT, done with Cyber-Tech and yes, done with my grandfather. I won't be used, Frank, and especially not by my own family. What he did was wrong and what's worse, he doesn't even care."

"But the COLT project's your life, it's who you are. You've always been so wrapped up in it all, so decisive, so self-assured. Wait, that's it."

"What's it?"

"What's so different about you."

"I'm different?" she asked, looking at him quizzically.

"You've changed. You just seem, well, you just seem more normal."

"More normal? Thanks, I think."

"No, I mean look at us," said Frank. "Look at the way we're talking right now. My whole time here and I was just another one of your subjects, designation COLT-45."

"I don't really think…"

"It was Russia," interrupted Frank looking

thoughtful. "Russia changed you."

"How do you mean?"

"You went into that building one person and came out another."

"Yes, I came out terrified."

"No, not that. It was the choice you made. Everyone in that meeting room knew I'd stolen the data, but still you defended me. Why?"

"I guess, well, I guess I just felt sorry for you," she replied.

"But why? I was only one of your subjects. I was just COLT-45."

"No, by then you were Frank Reynolds," she answered.

"See, I rest my case." Helena seemed lost in her own thoughts until finally, Frank broke the silence. "So doctor, what's next for you?"

"To be honest, I really don't know. Take one day at a time I suppose. What about you?"

"Part of me wants to go upstairs and make your grandfather pay for what he did. But, well, I keep telling myself I got what I came for," replied Frank, lifting his fists and morphing them into two small cannons.

"You okay in there Dr Brown?" asked a disembodied voice.

Helena smiled. "You might want to put those away Frank, you're scaring the staff."

Frank couldn't help but smile too as he morphed his hands back to normal.

"No pain?" asked Helena, already knowing the answer.

"Nope, another benefit of Russia I suppose," he said. "Any ideas?"

"Just a best guess I'm afraid. After the Cortex overloaded, we think your brain was given a choice. It either accepts the Cortex for what it is, or rejects it for good."

"Sounds pretty terminal."

"Yes, it would have been."

"See, you wouldn't have told me stuff like that before. Like I said, you've changed."

"Perhaps you're right."

"Anyway, looks like I've changed too," he answered, staring at his fists and thinking, of the weapons he'd achieved in Russia, "and it's certainly for the better."

Helena couldn't help but sigh. "Still about the weapons, Frank?"

"What else is there?" he replied quietly, still staring at his fists and missing the look of pity that crossed Helena's face.

"Look, before I go, just tell me one last thing. What really happened to the other COLT subjects?"

Helena took off her glasses and remained silent; leaving Frank wondering if she'd even heard him.

"Okay, I guess you've earned the right to know," she finally said.

Christ, how bad could this be? he thought, unsure whether he wanted to hear this now or not.

"The first COLTs were numbered one through fifteen. "We used monkeys from research labs and the initial trials went well. After successful limb replacements for all the subjects, we switched on the Cortices and, well, within a day they were all dead. Under-developed brains we thought, and so quickly moved onto human trials. We were confident things would work this time and so COLT-16 through

COLT-26 were all paid volunteers. Unfortunately for us, the people we got were vagrants, users and addicts. Their bodies rejected the Cortex and they too all died. We argued this was because their brains were in poor condition and Grandfather wanted to pull the plug, but I wasn't ready to give up just yet. I persuaded him to let me have one last go and we made the decision to use prisoners. Before you say it, yes, it was a terrible thing to do. But these were bad men; men already on death row and you have to understand, I was desperate, desperate to prove my theory worked."

"So what happened?" asked Frank with a degree of dread.

"Everyone died," whispered Helena looking at the floor. "COLT-44 was the last to go and I was left both devastated and defeated. I knew my Cortex worked, but it was always the same problem. The human brain just couldn't handle it."

"But for some reason my Cortex works?" asked Frank.

"Yes, and if I'm being honest, we don't know why."

Despite these revelations, Frank tried not to judge her too harshly. After all, he'd done things in his own past that would make experimenting on convicted murderers look tame. "Look, I appreciate your honesty Helena, but I still think you should have told me all this at the start."

"Yes, I know that now," she sighed.

"So, I'd be right in saying CCR were trying this too?"

Helena nodded, knowing full well what Frank was going to ask next.

"Did it work?"

"Unless we find a way to read that stolen data, I guess we'll never know for sure. Sorry Frank, but it looks like you're one of a kind."

Frank wasn't sure what to say to that.

Helena smiled as she stood up from the bed. "Anyway, you ready to go yet?"

As he looked around his room one last time, Frank felt a strange mix of emotions. Had he really gained anything from Cyber-Tech? What good were his weapons without an enemy to fight? Five minutes later, as he stood outside in the cool Chicago night air, he was thinking of his family again.

<><><>

Somewhere in northern Russia, a fire burned. Its flames were smaller now, but little remained of what had once been the headquarters of Cyber Corp Russia. Apart from the occasional explosion somewhere far underground, there was now a strange quiet to the devastation, a quiet that was suddenly broken by the ringing of a cell phone.

The sound continued until, as abruptly as it had started, it fell silent again. There then came a voice...

"Err... message for Dr Helena Brown... this is Harry... err... you know, Harry from accounts, err... anyway... call me when you can please... thanks... bye... CLICK"

At that point the battery died and, but for the ringing, the phone might have remained hidden amongst the rubble for centuries. But something had heard it. The sound of a human voice triggered impulses deep within the damaged circuits of a highly sophisticated processor. From there, millions of signals were quickly sent forth, gradually bringing systems back online and, as sensors suddenly came to life, emotions began to flow. It began with confusion, quickly followed by understanding, and then, finally, anger.

Rubble burst skywards as a scorched, metallic arm punched upwards from its shallow grave. Then came another arm, slowly followed by a huge, humanoid-shaped body. Reaching the surface, the creature followed its internal mapping across the ruined landscape to the point where it had triangulated the voice. It picked up the phone. Broken commands and sporadic programming clouded its thoughts, but one path was clear. In order to find those responsible, he must start with someone called Helena Brown.

CHAPTER NINE

The picture dominated his office and Johan Larrouy often found his eyes drawn towards it. He allowed himself a small smile. The picture was an enlarged cover of TIME magazine, one that had been originally published over forty years ago with the bold headline 'CYBER-TECH RISING.' Beneath that were the words 'Johan Larrouy - Back From Exile and Ready For Business!' Impressive as that statement was, it was the photograph that he really loved. His own younger self stood grinning outwards, dressed in a black tuxedo and looking for everything like he owned the world. One arm leant against the Ferrari parked next to him, whilst his other held what was actually the photograph's most noticeable subject. Even then, at three years of age, his daughter had the most incredible smile. It seemed to almost fill the page as she leant forwards in her father's arms, grinning at the camera. The cover story might have been about him, but Larrouy knew it was his daughter that had made it a sell-out issue. Turning his eyes from the image, he looked across his office towards the old meeting table and suddenly, memories came flooding back.

"You can all relax now, I'm back," said the young man, walking into the room in a brightly coloured tee-shirt and shorts. It wasn't just his clothing, but the long hair and sun-browned skin that made him look completely out of place. The other four men were all smartly dressed in expensive suits and were staring at him in amazement. "And it's probably a good thing too," he went on. "As it seems you've run my father's company into the ground."

George Overton was Cyber-Tech's Senior Director and he'd known Johan Larrouy since the day he was born. In fact, if he recalled correctly, he was actually his godfather and so it was with a somewhat forced smile that he stood up to respond.

"Johan, it's good to see you back. Now whilst you've been away enjoying yourself, some of us have been trying to keep this company afloat. I think we'd all agree it's probably best leaving the running of Cyber-Tech to us." As he sat down again, the other men nodded in agreement.

"Is that a fact?" replied Johan with a grin. "Well, perhaps you can tell me how, since my father's death, Cyber-Tech's market value has slid by an average of sixteen percent per year?"

"Actually…"

"Future orders stand at zero. Production lines close in three months and perhaps worst of all, the coffee machine in the foyer doesn't appear to be working."

"None of that…"

"And despite all of this," interrupted Johan, his grin taking on a slightly more sinister air, "you guys somehow get to live like kings on my father's money."

"What the hell are you talking about Johan? This isn't one of your childish games, this is business," said another of the older men.

"Yes, one you don't appear to be very good at."

"And you've got all the answers?" asked Overton.

"Indeed I have."

"Well in that case Johan, we'd love to know your plans on how we compete with the Chinese?"

"Easy, we start production of our own X-72 motherboards."

"Now, why didn't we think of that?" replied Overton, his voice heavy with sarcasm. "Be realistic Johan. To produce that level of technology we'd need access to their design specs."

"Actually, no we don't. We just copy the originals."

"Copy the originals? Do you honestly think we haven't thought of that? What you're suggesting is impossible; we'd need to somehow get hold of the original microchips."

"Nothing's impossible," answered Johan, throwing a handful of chips across the table. The four men looked at the scattered microchips in shock, which quickly turned to worry as a group of Cyber-Tech's security guards suddenly entered the room and took up positions beside Johan.

Overton smiled. "What do you want Johan?"

"What do I want? Well for a start, I want my father's business back."

"That's not going to happen."

"Secondly, I want his money back and before you say something you'll regret, you might want to hear me out. Despite the damage you've done to Cyber-Tech, I'm still willing to make you a deal. You accept a very generous redundancy package and I'll ensure that the FBI drop all charges against you."

"What charges?"

"You really need to ask?"

"No way Johan, not a chance," replied Overton angrily. "You must think we're mad."

Johan turned towards the nearest guard, a young man of about his own age. "What's your name kid?"

"Slade, sir."

"Well Slade, looks to me like Georgie-Boy's anger got the better of him. Good job you were here to protect me. Shoot him in the leg please."

Slade drew his weapon.

"You wouldn't dare…"

BANG.

Overton dropped like a stone as the bullet shattered his femur.

"Anyone else want to negotiate terms?"

The three men shook their heads and, as a pair of security guards picked up the moaning Overton, they quickly filed out of the room.

A few minutes later a young girl came running into the room. With a huge smile, she jumped up into her father's arms.

"Who were those old men?" she asked. "Was one of them hurt?"

"Don't worry about them babes. They were nothing but the past."

"Wow, look at the view!" she cried, wriggling out

of her father's arms and charging off towards the huge, panoramic windows.

"Nothing but the past…"

A knock at the door interrupted his thoughts. One of Larrouy's personal aides entered the room and hurried towards him looking pale.

"Sir, something's come up," began the nervous man, stopping behind Larrouy's imposing desk.

"Well, what is it?" asked Larrouy sharply.

"The object, the one we've been tracking, sir."

"Go on…"

"It's heading for Chicago."

So, it's finally made the connection, thought Larrouy with a smile. "Keep tracking it," he ordered, standing up.

"Yes sir," replied the aide, already turning to go.

"… and prepare my helicopter."

"Of course, sir."

"Oh, one last thing. Tell Slade to bring all his men in."

CHAPTER TEN

Frank Reynolds stood alone in the small cemetery. Before him were two gravestones, all that remained of his small family. It didn't make sense. Why was he still living and breathing, whilst those he was supposed to have taken care of were dead and buried? Even now, after all this time, he still felt so helpless. Lara had been his soul mate. He owed her everything and now she was gone forever. How was that fair?

They'd first met about a year after he joined the Chicago Police Department. He'd originally signed onto the force to help distance himself from the past; reasoning a 'stable' job like police work might be the change he needed after a lifetime of secrecy, warfare and death. But he soon found depressing similarities. Asked to 'turn a blind eye' once too often, Frank quickly found himself becoming disillusioned with life all over again. It was then, when he'd really hit rock bottom, that he'd found Lara.

She was doing temp work around the city and, as

fate would have it, had picked up a job within the admin department of the CPD. Frank had been ordered there to pick up his discharge papers and it was Lara who'd actually handed them over. Even now, after all this time, he could still remember the moment she walked into that waiting room.

"So you're leaving us," said the attractive woman, passing Frank his forms. "Mind telling me why?"
"Err," began Frank, somewhat taken aback. "I've got my reasons."
"Such as?" she replied, moving a chair to sit down next to him.
"Wait a minute… are you from Internal Affairs?" asked Frank, growing suspicious.
"Is that a pop group?"
"Err, no…" At that point Frank noticed the beginnings of a smile on her face. She was teasing him.
"I'm sorry," she said with a smile. "Sometimes I forget I'm supposed to take this more seriously. I'm Lara by the way," she said holding out her hand. "I'm new here."
"No kidding," he replied with a grin and they both burst out laughing.

Exactly a year to the day after they'd first met, Frank and Lara were married at a small service in the CPD Chapel. Yes, it was safe to say that Lara came into Frank's life like a hurricane and after the dust had settled, he was a different man, a better man.

Memories like these didn't help much now, but Frank had learned to harden himself to them. *What would you think of me now Lara?* he asked himself. *Would you even recognise the man you loved? A robotic freak, living only for revenge...* Frank looked down at the smaller gravestone and any thoughts of quitting left him immediately. Aayla had died too young and somehow, TALIR would pay.

"One day of freedom," began Frank, speaking aloud, "and Cyber-Tech want me back already?"

"I don't work there anymore, Frank," replied Helena softly.

"Sure, I remember why now. Mass murder just wasn't your thing, was it?"

"That's not fair, Frank."

"You're right," he said turning to face her. "Sorry, that was a low blow." He noticed she was holding a small cardboard box in her arms.

"Some of your stuff from COLT. Wasn't sure if you wanted it or not."

"Thanks," replied Frank, taking it from her with a small smile.

"Look, do you want to get a coffee or something? Okay, so maybe you want to just be left alone. You know what, this was probably a bad idea anyway," she stuttered, before being interrupted by her phone. "That's strange," she began, frowning at her phone's screen.

"What is?"

"Whoever's calling me, they're using my old cell phone."

"That's strange?"

"Sure it is, I lost it in Russia when…"

Frank snatched the phone out of her hands with a metallic fist, and immediately crushed it to pieces.

"Frank! What the hell are you doing?"

"Someone's trying to trace you," he answered,

looking around cautiously and fearing the worst.

THUUUUUUMPPHH!

The ground shook. Across the cemetery, Frank saw a large dust cloud billowing upwards. Something huge had hit the earth, gauging its way across the grassy field before eventually coming to rest there. Through the slowly clearing dust, Frank noticed a shape emerging.

"Run," he said, turning towards Helena. "Quickly, find somewhere to hide."

"What is that thing?" she asked, staring at what appeared to be an oversized robot. Suddenly her eyes widened. "No, it couldn't be..." she began, but before she could say any more, explosions started to rock the cemetery.

"RUN!" screamed Frank, forcibly pushing her away and, raising his arms, he turned to face the creature. The change came more easily now. With a simple thought, both of his arms began to grow in length and then widen, morphing and changing into rocket launchers. Each one was capable of sending high explosive shells onto targets well over a mile away. Frank stood and watched the creature approach. Its initial barrage had fallen short; the only damage was towards the far end of the cemetery and it hadn't fired again since. Frank wanted to make sure Helena was clear before he returned fire; he also wanted to get a closer look at what he was facing.

When he'd first seen it materializing from the dust, he'd assumed it was some kind of military robot, but now, as it strode towards him, he knew that wasn't entirely true. The creature had a human face, the pale, white flesh standing out in stark contrast to the dark materials covering the rest of its body. *It looks robotic*, thought Frank with growing unease, *but what if it's more than that?*

About fifty yards away the creature stopped moving. Frank watched in awe as its arms changed, each one morphing into a different weapon. At that moment, he knew he was no longer one of a kind. Wherever this cyborg had come from, it had attacked first and that made it an enemy. Checking Helena had left the cemetery, Frank lifted his arms and fired an opening salvo towards the massive creature. He braced himself as a dozen small rockets arced upwards out of his arms, each one powerful enough to halt something twice the creature's size. *Let's see how he copes with that,* he thought with an odd sense of pleasure. It felt good to be using his weaponry at last and, as the rockets detonated, obliterating the area around the cyborg, Frank finally felt the true power of his technology.

"That should slow you down a bit," he said with grin, one that quickly disappeared as striding towards him and apparently unaffected by several hundred pounds of high explosives, the cyborg continued its advance. Frank could see its face in detail now and was shocked to see it was smiling. *Whatever it is,* he thought, *it must have been human once. Could it be reasoned with?* Frank decided he had to at least try.

"Wait!" he called, holding up his weaponized arms in a gesture of peace. "I don't know what you want, but let's talk about…"

POP… CRUUUMP!

Frank didn't even see the attack coming. One second he was talking and the next he was on his back. *Jesus, he's fast, I don't stand a chance.* Sitting up, Frank felt a stinging pain across his chest. He knew he'd taken shrapnel, but thankfully his metallic legs had sustained most of the damage and they were strong enough to do so.

POP…

This time Frank was moving. Before the mortar had even landed, he'd dived for cover behind the nearest gravestone. He felt the explosion hit and then, without waiting, he moved again. Just because the cyborg could fire its weapons quickly, that didn't mean it could react quickly too. As Frank ducked behind another large gravestone, he risked a look and saw that he might have guessed right. Now a few dozen yards away, he could see just how huge the cyborg really was. It had reached the surrounding wall of the cemetery and, standing over fifteen feet tall, it seemed cumbersome and hampered by its own weight. Watching it attempt to lift one of its massive legs over the wall, Frank knew he must use this knowledge to his advantage if he was going to survive. He had to keep moving. He had to outpace the creature, force it to manoeuver before it could take aim. The cyborg now had one leg over the wall and Frank took another chance. He darted out from behind the grave and fired off a small salvo of rockets. This time they had an effect. Unable to defend itself properly from the unexpected attack, the cyborg was hit by several blasts and Frank saw that it had at least been damaged. The creature swung its huge arms towards him, but Frank was on the move again, looking for a way to somehow circle around behind it. Once again, his plan seemed to be working, as the giant creature wasn't able to track Frank quickly enough to fire. *That's it*, thought Frank eagerly, *that's the answer. Don't let it get into a position where it can…*

BOOM!

Frank went crashing to the ground, his head narrowly missing the sharp corner of a raised tombstone. As he lifted himself up he began to feel faint and, glancing at his side, saw his shirt was in tatters. Stretching across his ribs was a deep cut and it was already bleeding heavily. *Damn*, he thought with a mixture of anger and surprise, *how the hell did it manage that?*

"Stay down," said a voice at his side.

Frank turned to see Helena kneeling beside him, peering out over the top of the tombstone.

"Helena? What the hell are you doing here?"

"Sorry Frank, but I've never been much of a spectator. Here, let's get you sitting upright." Frank winced as she helped him up.

"Where is it?" he asked.

"It's over the wall," she replied, quickly ducking down again before the creature could spot her.

"You need to leave right now Helena."

"From what I can tell," she began, ignoring his words, "it's favouring its right arm and there must be a good reason for that." She quickly tore a sleeve from her shirt top and used it to bind Franks wound. "I'm guessing each arm has its own separate programming. Right one for speed and left for something else, something like power or range."

"You're guessing?"

"Yes, I'm guessing," she replied, hastily finishing the bandage at his side. "You got any better ideas?"

Frank couldn't help but smile. "I suppose it'll have to do for now. Right, stay low, I'm going to try and take that right arm out." With a grimace, Frank shuffled himself into a kneeling position and then cleared his mind. Asking the Cortex for something specific was not something he'd ever tried before. *No time like the present*, he thought with a bitter smile. Frank watched as his arm changed. It grew longer, before narrowing into a thin tube. A weapon not designed for firing mortars or rockets, but for something much more precise. Slowly, he lifted the electron-pulse rifle around the side of the gravestone and took aim at the cyborg's head. But would a head shot even work? Somehow Frank doubted it; no, he had to stick to the original plan. If he could take out the favoured arm, then he might, just might, have a chance.

Suddenly the cyborg spotted him. It started to swing its arm towards his hiding place and Frank knew he'd run out of time; it was now or never. The electron-pulse fired and Frank watched as the charge hit the creature's outstretched arm just moments before it could use its own weapon. A surge of electrical energy wrapped itself around the cyborg's metallic arm and then, with a loud crack, it dropped to hang uselessly by its side. Before Frank could even smile, the creature was swinging its other arm towards him and he'd no choice but to duck for cover.

"Stay down," he shouted and they braced for the incoming rounds. Time seemed to slow, but it was still several seconds before they heard the explosions. Frank turned to look at Helena who was smiling. "Looks like you were right. Response time's down, which must mean it's slower with that arm."

Helena chanced another look over the grave and saw the creature once again striding towards them. "Come on, we've got to go," she said. Helping Frank to his feet, they both darted across the graveyard, all the while keeping as low to the ground as possible.

Frank was now heavily reliant on Helena for support as they made their way back through the cemetery as far as the old church. Beyond that point, there was little by way of cover or places to hide. *I can't keep this up*, he thought with growing desperation. *I need to end this… alone.*

"Stay here," he said suddenly.

"No Frank, I'm not leaving you."

But he'd made his decision. If Frank could somehow lead the cyborg back across the cemetery, she might just get the chance to escape.

Helena must have realized what he was planning. "No Frank!" she pleaded.

He jumped to his feet and darted out from behind the church wall. Gathering speed, he began to run back across the cemetery.

KA-BOOM!

Frank felt himself spin through the air, before crashing down against the side of the church. Then everything went black.

When he came around, Helena was once again at his side. He tried to sit up… and realized that something was very wrong. *What the hell…?* Frank looked down to see his right arm had been torn off below the shoulder. All that remained was a mess of twisted metal, still somehow attached to his body. With rising panic, he tried to morph what was left of the arm, but there was nothing, no response at all.

"Jesus," he whispered.

"Frank, listen to me," said Helena, gently turning his head to face her own. "Use your rockets. Change your legs and get out of here."

"I can't carry you like this," he replied, pointing

towards the mangled remains of his right arm.

"I'm not asking you to."

"No way," he replied, already shaking his head. "I'm not leaving you here by yourself."

"Frank, you've got no choice. You need to think…"

"Forget it Helena, just help me to my feet."

Fighting off a growing nausea and with Helena's help, he eventually managed to get himself upright. "Where's it gone? Can you still see it?" he asked, looking about with blurred vision.

"It's coming," was her simple reply.

"Then get out of here, please. I don't understand what you're even doing here."

"That's it!" said Helena suddenly, her face brightening.

"What's it?"

"We've got to try something it doesn't understand. Remember, it's a machine. It's controlled by its software. Confuse that programming and we might just have a chance."

"So what do we do?"

"I… I don't know," she admitted.

"Well," replied Frank slowly, "I reckon I do." It was a desperate gamble and the odds were against him, but he'd nothing left. This would be the last throw of the dice.

"Frank, what are you doing?"

"Wish me luck," he said with a smile before turning and running straight at the cyborg.

Frank covered the ground quickly and, as he'd hoped, the creature didn't seem to understand this sudden change of tactics. It opened fire with a rapidly morphed chain gun, but the rounds went wild as

Frank narrowed the distance between them in seconds. Whatever the cyborg's true history, whatever its training or programming, Frank prayed that close quarter combat hadn't been a part of it. Leaping high into the air with robotic enhanced limbs, he morphed his remaining hand into a blade before coming crashing down on top of the cyborg. His momentum alone drove the blade cleanly through its chest and as they tumbled to the ground, he quickly rolled clear. Whether he had hit anything vital, Frank couldn't tell, but the cyborg was grounded, though Frank didn't know for how long. He had to act fast. With an instant command to his Cortex, his bladed arm morphed into a hollow, glowing tube before he lowered it to point at the downed creature's chest.

"No! Don't destroy it!" came a shout from somewhere behind him. Frank recognized the voice and with a small smile, chose to ignore it. Dozens of small limpet mines shot out of his arm and attached themselves across the metallic parts of the cyborg's body. Frank waited for the creature to move, or at least to try and defend itself, but instead, he watched as its pale face turned towards him. Their eyes locked and, for a moment, Frank thought he saw something like gratitude there.

Backing slowly away, he watched in silence as a series of rapid explosions reduced the cyborg to pieces

Had he done the right thing? Suddenly Frank wasn't so sure and, as he limped off, he felt his anger mount. His battle with the cyborg might be over, but he knew another was about to start. It took a lot of self-control, but somehow Frank managed to keep his feelings in check.

"You've got a lot of nerve coming here," he said, stopping before Johan Larrouy.

"Frank," began Larrouy warmly, "don't be like that. It wasn't my fault the Russian data got messed up."

"To hell with the data! You murdered hundreds of innocent people!"

"Innocent were they? Just who do you think made that?" replied Larrouy, nodding towards the remains of the cyborg.

"That doesn't make it right, Larrouy and you know it," growled Frank, pushing past the big man and walking painfully away. He wasn't in the mood for Johan Larrouy or his games. His body ached and his side was still bleeding. All he wanted to do was to get away, away from everyone and everything.

"So tell me Frank," continued Larrouy regardless. "How much do you know about Jacob Barlow?"

Frank stopped in his tracks. "Everything," he replied through gritted teeth, "and if you mention his name again, I'll kill you."

"Barlow wasn't the bomber, Frank. The man who killed your family was called Jacob Canagan."

Frank stopped again. "I know that name," he replied softly.

Got him, thought Larrouy, trying hard not to smile. "And so you should Frank, considering you were in Delta together for almost five years."

Frank turned slowly around. "You're telling me that Jake Canagan joined TALIR and then what, blew himself up for them? Sorry Larrouy, but I find that pretty hard to believe."

"I'm afraid it's the truth."

"Then who's Barlow? Why's his name linked to the bombing?"

"He's nobody, at least nobody important. It was probably just some name they used to cover everything up."

"So now it's a cover up? This is getting worse, Larrouy. You're saying the police, the FBI, hell, even the government are involved?"

"Think about it, Frank. A highly-decorated soldier like Canagan choses to murder innocent people, innocent American people. Well, that's no end of bad PR. The military wanted to keep it under wraps and so they did. The easiest thing to do was cover up the bomber's real name and blame it on someone else."

Was there actually something to this? It might explain why he'd never got very far with his own investigations. He needed the truth, but first, he had to play the big man at his own game. "Okay Larrouy, so let's say I believe you. What's all this to you? Why this sudden revelation?"

"Frank, the man who killed your family was an old friend. Is that a coincidence?"

"You're not answering the question," replied Frank, straining to keep calm, "and I'm starting to get annoyed."

Larrouy stood his ground with a smile, but before anything could happen, Helena came running up. She was closely followed by several very flustered looking aides.

"Sorry sir," began one of them. "She refused to stay put."

Larrouy didn't take his eyes off Frank, and sensing the tension, Helena immediately placed herself between them. With a stern glance at her grandfather, she turned to face Frank.

"Frank, you're hurt. Why don't we get you back to the lab and fix that arm?"

"Back to Cyber-Tech? No, I don't think so Dr Brown," he answered, continuing to stare daggers at Larrouy as he weighed up what to do next.

"Your move Frank," said Larrouy calmly.

"You and me, we aren't finished," said Frank. As he turned to leave, he staggered, fighting to keep himself upright and then suddenly Helena was at his side. With her help, he managed to keep walking towards the waiting helicopter, his mind still reeling. *What if Larrouy was telling the truth? Could Jake Canagan really be the bomber?*

More helicopters landed nearby and Frank spotted Swamps jumping out of one of them with his men. As the well-armed group reached Larrouy, the small man gave Frank a quick grin, one which quickly disappeared when Frank pointed his still morphed weapon at his face.

"What now boss?" Swamps asked Larrouy. "We just let them go?"

"Yes," answered the larger man quietly. "Now we wait."

CHAPTER ELEVEN

When Johan Larrouy entered the COLT lab, he was pleased to see it was a hive of activity. Scientists and technicians scurried about the large room, all engrossed in various tasks and all desperate to make the restarted project a success. Commendable as that was, Larrouy wanted results and he was here to see if Crawford had any.

"Dr Crawford," he said, entering the tall man's office and closing the door behind him. "Tell me how the Russians came to be using AI brains."

"Well, I'm not sure where to start, sir," replied Crawford, rising from behind his computer terminal and looking like he hadn't slept for days. "The fact that CCR were even using Artificial Intelligence came as a surprise. When we learnt they'd got their AIs up to level fifty, we were stunned."

"Get to the point," said Larrouy. "Did they work or not?"

"Their data suggests an eighty to ninety percent

success rate for all cortex activations," replied Crawford looking awestruck. "It's unprecedented."

"So what's the problem? Can't we just copy their design?" asked Larrouy.

"There's nothing to copy. The stolen data talks of a new kind of processor but gives few details. We think CCR got them from China and that obviously rules out getting some of our own. Without these processors, our own AIs won't get past level forty."

"And that's not high enough?"

"No sir, they won't accept the Cortex."

"What if we had one of these Russian AIs?"

"Well, it'd have to be alive to be of any use and there's not much chance of that with their base destroyed."

Larrouy smiled at the doctor's discomfort. "Bring it in," he ordered, now talking into his wrist communicator. One of the service lifts at the far end of the lab opened and everyone watched as Swamps wheeled in a crate full of robotic parts.

"What's all this?" asked Crawford.

"Something that escaped the destruction of the Russian base. We've been tracking it a while now."

Crawford strode towards the crate. "What happened to it?"

"COLT-45 happened to it," replied Larrouy looking irritated, but Crawford wasn't listening any more.

Taking the cyborg's head off the trolley, he quickly set it down on a nearby workbench and, as Larrouy watched, the doctor carefully unscrewed the fastenings around a metallic plate covering its skull.

"Yes! It's a level fifty and it's still intact," cried Crawford, unable to hide his excitement after lifting the plate clear. "But we're running out of time. You and you," he said, pointing at two of his nearest staff. "Take this up to the Cryo lab and be quick about it. I'll be there shortly; I just need to get my notes."

As the scientists carefully carried the cyborg's head away, Crawford rushed back to his office, Larrouy following behind.

"So, it's definitely one of theirs?" he asked.

"Yes sir and, more importantly, it's still alive," answered Crawford with a grin. "I should have the processor design copied by the end of the week," he continued, shuffling through the paperwork on his desk. "I just need to find my notes and then…"

"The brain can wait, doctor," interrupted Larrouy.

"But, sir…"

"I said it can wait."

"But…" began Crawford before the look in Larrouy's eyes silenced him immediately.

"There's a little something I need you to do first," said Larrouy with a smile.

It had only taken Helena a few hours to fix Frank's arm. Thankfully, he hadn't needed anything in the way of complicated surgery. Morphing a new limb from his damaged one, Helena had waited patiently for him to speak. Still silent after all the final tests were complete, she decided he probably wasn't going to start by himself.

"So Frank. What now?"

"Jacob Canagan," was his simple answer.

"Who's he?"

"That's exactly what I intend to find out," he replied, rising from his seat and striding for the door.

"Frank, before you go…"

He stopped and looked back at her, grey eyes now cold and haunted.

"Look, you probably don't remember this," she began. "But we've met before." When he didn't reply, Helena carried on regardless. "It was about seven or eight years ago. You freed a group of kids being held at the City Museum and I was one of them. I think back to that day now and I wish... well, I wish I could start again. I'd do things differently."

"Apology accepted," said Frank and without another world, he strode from the room leaving Helena staring after him.

A short time later and Helena was sat in the back of an Auto Taxi feeling completely confused about the direction her life was now taking. Just when she had thought herself free of Cyber-Tech, the decision to check up on Frank Reynolds had, somewhat incredibly, resulted in her return. Crawford was now running COLT and he'd taken great pleasure when she'd asked him permission to fix Frank's arm. Denied access to the main labs, Helena got the impression something was going on in there, which struck her as strange coming so soon after COLT-45's departure. *He's Frank, not COLT-45*, she thought to herself with some disgust. *I guess you've not changed that much after all. Maybe you're always destined to be that spoilt little rich girl...*

Helena smiled as an idea suddenly struck her. "Change of plan. Take me to Forty-First Street," she said into the Auto Taxi's communicator.

"Yes ma'am," came the computerised response.

Time for some advice, she though still smiling, *and for once, I might actually listen to him.*

<><><>

It was late afternoon and most of his lunchtime regulars had drifted away. A little early for the night time crowd, Bix had always liked this strange transition period between drinking groups. As he leant on the long, wooden bar top, he knew he was already drunk. Some would call it unprofessional, but Roadhouse was his bar and he reckoned he could do as he liked. Besides, he wasn't actually on duty for another hour and Phoenix always kept his glass full. *Which is probably why I keep her on*, he thought with a smile. *It wasn't for her interpersonal skills, that was for sure.* As if on cue, the flame-haired barmaid grunted something unintelligible and nodded towards the door where a young woman had just walked in. She looked wealthy and was well-dressed, entirely inappropriate for the kind of establishment he ran. The court order preventing them being in the same room also told Bix something must be wrong.

"The last time I came here," began the young woman, crossing the almost deserted room to sit on a barstool next to Bix, "I had to wear a black wig, leather jacket and an awful lot of studs."

"Can't say it suited you either, but at least no one knew who you were. What are you doing here Helena? Are you trying to get me into trouble?"

"I've just got off the phone to the solicitors. Apparently the fact my mother hasn't updated the injunction in the last three years means it's no longer valid."

"So I don't have to wear a disguise to see my daughter anymore?"

Helena laughed. "I was the one who had to wear all those silly clothes. The only disguise you do is 'Old Hippy Rocker' and that's permanent."

"I'll take that as a compliment," he replied, standing from his stool to give her a hug. "Still, it must be pretty serious for you to come here. I'm sure your grandfather wouldn't approve."

"Well, for a start he can go to hell and secondly, I need some advice."

"Advice from me?" he laughed. "I'm probably the last person you should listen to. Made a complete mess of my life, wouldn't want you doing the same thing hun."

Helena looked at her father. He was now in his late fifties, had long grey hair tied back in a ponytail, a beard that was thick and unruly and if she guessed correctly, he was probably drunk. It was hard recognizing him as the same man who stood centre stage in the huge poster that covered an entire end of the room.

Bix saw her glance at the poster. "I had it all once, but you know that don't you? When your mother came along... well, everything changed."

"We've spoken about this before Dad. It wasn't your fault."

"Thanks for saying so hun, but you're wrong." His eyes too drifted towards the huge poster. The photograph showed his band in their heyday nearly thirty years ago. It was taken during a live performance at the White House, not long after they'd received their fifth Grammy. The guitar he held in his hands was mounted over the bar, just another bit of memorabilia like the rest spread about the room. "That's where I met your mother," he said with a smile, nodding at the poster. "But you know the rest, don't you?"

"Sure, after she got pregnant, grandfather destroyed your life."

"I suppose he was only trying to protect her. Could you really see it? Pamela Larrouy, daughter of the great Johan Larrouy, living the seedy life of a rock star groupie? Nope, that was never going to happen."

"Maybe not, but that didn't give him the right to do what he did." Helena sighed. "I guess destroying people's lives is what he's good at."

"Now that sounds serious. Want a drink?"

Helena nodded and Bix called for two scotches. They arrived with a grunt from Phoenix and he watched as Helena took a mouthful. After a small splutter and with a definite grimace, she eventually swallowed the liquid.

"Christ," she said in a deep voice. "How the hell can you drink that stuff?"

"Because I'm a rock star," replied her dad with a grin. Helena laughed and took another swig.

"Well," she began. "You were right, things have been pretty serious recently. I've left Cyber-Tech and I won't be going back in a hurry."

"What about your COLT project? I thought working on that for Cyber-Tech was all you ever wanted?"

"It was, but God help me, there's a dark side to it, one that finally raised its head in Russia. Something happened to me over there Dad, something that made me realize a few things about myself and when I got back, I was changed... changed for the better."

"Sounds like a good start, so what's the problem?"

"I can't escape the past."

"That thing at the cemetery?"

"What? How'd you know about that?"

"Saw some footage of Cyber-Tech helicopters and your grandfather's name was mentioned. Wondered if you were involved."

"Involvement is something of an understatement. Look Dad, I'm trying to help someone, but all I seem to do is make things worse. I'm the one responsible for getting him into this mess and I just want to make things right. But... but I don't know how."

Bix nodded slowly. "When I was alienated from your family, I took rejection badly. I was one of the most famous musicians on the planet, but judged unfit for your mother. I grew bitter, then angry and finally hit the bottle harder than I'd ever done before. I destroyed my own career, not your grandfather. I refused to accept what was happening. I took the wrong path."

"Am I taking the right path Dad?"

"Have you changed?"

"Yes."

"Do you feel better about yourself?"

Helena nodded.

"Then, sounds to me like you're already there," he replied with a smile.

"But it's just so difficult..." she began, before being interrupted by her phone. Taking it out of her pocket, she looked at the caller's name and with a shrugged apology, answered it. The conversation was short, but afterwards Helena found herself smiling.

"Your friend?" asked her dad.

"Yes, he wants my help."

"Not that difficult after all," Bix said with a grin as Phoenix poured him another drink.

CHAPTER TWELVE

It still took Frank almost two days to track down and arrange a meeting with the man he hoped could provide those answers. He'd then called Helena and asked if she'd go with him. Frank was hoping she might hear something he'd missed, or perhaps just see things from a different angle. Whatever the reason, he had been glad when she'd said yes.

"So this person we're meeting, Harwood, he was in Delta with you and Canagan?" asked Helena in between sips of her coffee. They were sat opposite each other at a corner table in an old style diner and the only other person in the room was a tired-looking waitress.

"Yes," he replied, pushing some soggy fries around his plate. "We were on the same team."

"So what makes you think he'll show up?"

"One thing you can say about Harwood, always reliable," answered Frank looking slightly lost in the past. Helena didn't want to push it any further and was about to change the subject when Frank started speaking again.

"There were four of us in the team and we were solid. Harwood was probably the best sniper in the division, Canagan handled explosives, Bert ran comms and I led the team. We did dozens of missions and, somehow, survived them all. Perhaps we were the best, perhaps we were just lucky… either way, we were like brothers, no, we were closer than brothers." Frank sighed and gave up on his fries. He briefly looked up at Helena.

"There was this one mission we did. We were deep behind enemy lines and waiting for the charges to blow. Problem was, we still hadn't heard back from Harwood. If he wasn't in position, we were in big trouble. Suddenly we heard his voice over the sat com. He said he was good to go and so when the explosives went off, we went in, knowing he had our backs. The mission was another success for Delta. Later, we discovered he'd taken out a sentry and got a knife in the stomach for the effort. I asked him why he hadn't aborted the mission, as was protocol, and his reply was simple. He couldn't let his team down. Our boss at that time was Major Frost and he immediately cited him for the Medal of Honour. Three weeks later Harwood was well enough to receive it from the president himself. That was the sort of team we were."

"Wow."

"Sorry," said Frank. "I've not really talked about stuff like that before."

"It's okay Frank," said Helena. "I said I wanted to help and I meant it, even if it's only to listen."

Frank looked into her eyes and saw the truth.

"Reynolds," said a heavyset man, appearing suddenly at their table with a welcoming smile.

"Hello Harwood," replied Frank, returning the grin. "Take a seat," he added, moving over slightly so his old friend could sit down. Helena noticed that Harwood was one of those men it was hard to age, the type who might be in their thirties, fifties, or anywhere in between.

"This is Helena," said Frank. "She's helping me out."

Harwood flashed her a smile. "So Frank, you wanted to talk to me."

"I need some information and… well, the police aren't being very helpful."

"I thought you were the police?"

"I was until my little accident." Frank lifted his metallic hands slightly.

"Ah yes, your cool-looking new limbs, all courtesy of Dr Brown here," said Harwood nodding towards her.

Be careful Frank, thought Helena suddenly. *He might be an old friend, but he's sharp.*

"Look, I'll get straight to the point. I need to know more about Jacob Canagan."

"Canagan? Sure, what's he got to do with anything?"

"I think he killed my family," replied Frank.

"Your family? But wasn't that the TALIR bombing?"

"Yes, and I know it's going to sound hard to believe, but I think he was the bomber."

Harwood was silent. After a short while, he began to speak softly. "Frank, I reckon you and your family were just in the wrong place at the wrong time."

"What the hell's that got to do with anything?" asked Frank, banging the table in frustration. "Dammit Harwood, you knew Canagan better than anyone. If he blew up my six-year-old daughter, I want to know why."

"Okay Frank I'll tell you what I know, but it's going to cause problems, big problems. You sure about this?"

Frank nodded. "Just tell me."

"Alright then, but don't say I didn't warn you," the big man replied before composing himself. "To tell you the truth, life after Delta was pretty tough for me and Canagan. Seemed neither of us could hold a job down. When I finally got some steady work, well, he was pretty deep into the bottle by then and I started to see less of him. Anyway, it must have been about a month before the bombing and, out of the blue, he turned up at my door. He looked to have straightened himself out, you know, full of confidence and jabbering about some big thing he was a part of. Told me he'd been chosen for something special."

"Jesus," said Frank looking pale.

"Asked me right then if I wanted to join him."

"What? Join TALIR?"

"Nope, he was talking about Delta."

"Delta? He was back in Delta?" asked Frank.

"Seems he never left."

"He never left? But… but if he was with Delta when the bomb exploded…"

"Then TALIR are using Delta to do their dirty work for them."

"Jesus Holy Christ. That can't possibly be true," said Frank, sitting back in his chair and feeling slightly sick.

"Frank, it's fifteen years since we left Delta and the world's changed a lot since then. We fought an old-style war against the Eastern States, but now it's all terrorists, splinter groups and private armies. Who better to run TALIR than Delta? The way they operate, it's practically the same thing."

"But why? Why do it? What's in it for Delta?"

"I don't know the answer to that one Frank and I don't want to. I like to keep myself clear of trouble these days, and I suggest you do the same."

"I wish I could," replied Frank.

"Look," began Harwood as he stood to leave. "I've probably said too much already, but I owe you Frank. You really want to know why Delta's running TALIR? Then start at the top; go for its cold-hearted leader." He turned and left as quickly as he'd arrived.

For a moment, Frank and Helena were left alone with their thoughts. Helena looked across at Frank and as she watched, his face slowly turned from confusion to understanding, and then anger. Suddenly he jumped up, his metallic arms ripping the table free from the floor. He hurled it across the room with a roar of pain and anguish. Helena shrank back in terror as she saw the look of rage in Frank's eyes. Without a word, Frank turned and ran out of the building. Helena got up to follow, but by the time she'd paid the ashen-faced waitress for the damage as well as for their coffees, Frank was long gone.

CHAPTER THIRTEEN

Frank left the diner raging against the world. At that moment, he was ready to morph his guns and face the man he now knew was responsible for the murder of his family. But a voice in his head urged caution. If he rushed into this without a plan, it would be suicide. Not only that, his death would be completely pointless. No one would be any the wiser about this terrible connection between TALIR and Delta. Frank forced himself to calm down and as he walked back to his apartment, gave himself time to think carefully.

It was obvious Harwood had gone out on a limb for him. He'd practically told Frank the name of the man running TALIR, but without actually mentioning it. Harwood had used the phrase 'cold-hearted leader' and that, in conjunction with his revelation about Delta, had led Frank to one simple conclusion. He was talking about a very specific person, their former commanding officer, Major Ryan Frost.

Frank and his team had often joked about their boss' name being well-suited. Major Frost had gained something of a cold-hearted reputation, mostly due to his willingness to get a job done whatever the cost. Much as Frank hated to believe Frost was involved, he couldn't discount the possibility, which was why he now sat waiting in an expensive ante-room outside his former boss's office.

"The colonel will see you now, Mr Reynolds," said the pretty receptionist, interrupting Frank's train of though. *A colonel already,* he thought, rising from the plush sofa. It was clear Frost's career had been kind to him, especially if working in this building was anything to go by. Officially it was part of Homeland Security, but after being led through numerous security checks and along countless corridors, Frank guessed there was probably more to it than that.

As he turned towards the large door, Frank suddenly felt very alone. Earlier that day, Helena had called and, after hearing what he planned to do, she'd immediately offered to accompany him. Frank had been tempted, but he knew this was something he had to do alone. Now, as he opened the door to Frost's office, he found himself wishing he'd asked her to come along after all.

Colonel Ryan Frost had indeed done well for himself. His office was both luxurious and modern. It was fitted with a multitude of display screens, all streaming images from a variety of sources such as CCTV, television news stations and satellite feeds. *Well, whatever Frost does for a living,* thought Frank, *there's a lot of money behind it.* The colonel was just coming off the phone as Frank entered and greeted him with a simple nod.

"Hello Frank," Frost said, remaining seated. "What can I do for you?"

Straight to the point as ever, thought Frank, *no change there then. Well, two can play at that game.*

"How long have you been running TALIR?" asked Frank calmly. If Colonel Frost was surprised at the accusation, it didn't show. He sat back in his chair and stared at Frank thoughtfully. Frank slowly counted to ten as a multitude of questions rushed through his head. *Would Frost deny it? How much did he really know? What was Delta's connection to TALIR?* Frank had taken a massive gamble by coming right out with the accusation, but knowing Frost the way he did, he thought it was probably his best shot.

"I'm sorry for your loss Frank, it was never part of the overall plan."

Frank was too stunned to speak. He'd expected denial, or even anger, but this?

"So, so you don't deny it?" he whispered, his throat suddenly dry.

"Why should I? Canagan worked for me and his mistake killed your family."

"You won't get away with this," said Frank, his calm now beginning to evaporate.

"I already have," replied Frost. "Look, I like you Frank, always did, but you've been digging too deep. You've left me no choice."

Frank had heard enough. With a simple command to his Cortex, his arms began to change. Fingers fused as metallic limbs hollowed into barrels. Electron rounds chambered, awaiting the mental trigger to send them screaming towards a target. As Frank stood there, arms pulsing with barely restrained power, Frost didn't even flinch.

"I'm afraid you're as good as dead, Frank, but involving that doctor? Well, that was just stupid."

"Leave her out of this, she's got nothing…"

"Nothing?" interrupted Frost.

Frank wasn't going to be baited. "Look, you're going down Frost. When this becomes public, you're finished."

"How? You won't be alive long enough to tell anyone."

"My death won't stop anything. Helena knows who to talk to and before you ask, she's safe."

"Got it all covered, haven't you?" asked Frost.

"I'd be stupid not to. Besides, she's not your only problem. If I don't come back, an old friend will know what to do."

"Yes, I'm sure he will," said Frost with a smile. Frank heard a door open behind him and turning, he watched in horror as Helena staggered into the room. Her mouth was gagged, her hands bound and she looked at him with eyes that were filled with fear

Frank's shock turned to anger as he saw who followed.

"So you're a part of this too?" he asked with a snarl, pointing one weaponized arm at Harwood, whilst keeping the other trained on Frost.

"Sorry Frank," replied Harwood, pushing Helena forwards with the end of his gun. "The plan was to bring you in too, but after your family got killed we knew that was never going to happen."

Stalemate, thought Frank grimly. "So what now?" he asked Frost.

"Well Frank, that depends on you… and of course Dr Brown here."

"She's got nothing to do with this. Let her go."

"That can be arranged."

"Okay Frost, let's hear it. What do you want?"

"I think you know the answer to that Frank. You go for a little ride with Harwood here."

"A one way ride," answered Frank. Behind Harwood, Helena was desperately shaking her head, eyes pleading with him not to do it.

Frank looked at her and smiled. Any advantage he'd had had disappeared the minute she'd walked through that door. Slowly lowering his weaponized arms, he morphed them back to normal and, as he did so, saw Helena's head slump forward in defeat.

"It's the only sensible thing to do, Frank," began Frost. "You've just saved…"

CRUNCH.

Harwood's nose exploded as Helena's head slammed backwards into it and, as the big man crumpled to the floor, both Frank and Frost looked on in some disbelief.

Suddenly Frost stood up. Frank saw him pull a gun from under his desk. Diving to one side, Frank's right arm became a machine pistol, spraying bullets towards his former boss before the man could even take aim. The rounds cut across Frost's legs, causing massive damage at short range and sending him sprawling to the floor. Frank quickly got back to his feet and, moving around the desk, he kept his arm trained on the now badly bleeding Colonel.

"How could you?" asked Frank sadly as he looked down upon his former boss. "How could you murder innocent people?"

Legs shattered, Frost's face was a wash of pain. "Just following orders, Frank," he replied with a small smile, before a ripple of agony turned it into a grimace.

"Whose orders?" demanded Frank.

"You really don't know?"

Frank stared at him wordlessly.

"America fights the terrorists, the terrorists fight back. The military get better weapons and so do they. It's called escalation Frank."

"And TALIR helps keep that escalation going."

"Smart boy Frank," replied Frost, turning paler by the second but still managing to smile.

Frank realized he was running out of time. "Dammit Frost, if you're not behind all this, then who is? I want names!"

"You want to know something else, Frank?" replied the Colonel. "We didn't just run TALIR... we ran all of them... every... last... one"

"Jesus," whispered Frank. Standing with his arm trained at Frost's chest, he knew the moment of his revenge was at hand. Everything had been leading up to this, but now it was finally here, he realized he wasn't done yet. He needed to understand.

"Please" said Frank softly. "For the sake of my family, just tell me what you know."

Frost was silent for so long that Frank thought he'd lost him.

"I... I had my own reasons for all of this. But there were others... other families... who did it for money and power. Isn't that right, Dr Brown?" he finished weakly, turning his head towards Helena who'd moved to stand behind them, gag removed.

Frank looked towards her and saw understanding there too.

"Let me speak to him first."

"And say what?"

"I... I don't know," replied Helena sadly.

"Do what you can for him," said Frank, looking down at his old boss with a mixture of pity and hatred. Then, morphing his hands back to normal, he hastily scribbled a note. "Give me an hour and then call this number. Tell them everything."

Helena could only nod. Words, it seemed, had failed her.

CHAPTER FOURTEEN

"This better work," said Larrouy, fixing Dr Crawford with a steely glare. The boss of Cyber-Tech was behind his large desk holding a small, black box in one hand.

"Well, it's not been field tested, but I can assure…"

"For your sake doctor, I hope you're right," interrupted Larrouy as he placed the small transmitter into his jacket pocket. "Now, tell me about the AI."

"We're making excellent progress," the tall doctor replied, his eyes lighting up with enthusiasm. "The brain's functioning well, and so far the data we've got…"

"Yes, yes, but is it ready for trials?"

"Maybe in a few weeks…"

"Too slow," interrupted Larrouy. "Dr Crawford, I'm placing you in charge of Cyber-Tech's biggest project to date, the Droid Organic Limb Trials. I want the Russian AIs compatible with our cyber-organics by the end of the week and I'm expecting the first of these DROLTs operational within three months."

"Three months!? But sir…"

"Do you want replacing?" said Larrouy with a cold smile, as he rose from his chair and turned to stare out over his city.

Crawford let himself out.

Frank Reynolds was going to die. Despite knowing this, he'd been pleasantly surprised to get this far with his plan. He'd simply walked into the Cyber-Tech building and asked to see Johan Larrouy. Several minutes later and he was riding the elevator to the top floor, personally escorted there by one of Larrouy's fawning aides. Frank was under no illusions that Larrouy knew why he was here. You didn't run a secret terrorist organisation like TALIR without having a firm grip on rapidly evolving situations. Situations like this, where Frank was here to single-handedly destroy the organisation from the top down. Still, he'd expected at least a little bit of rough treatment, rather than a personal escort to the man he was here to kill.

When the elevator doors opened, a tall, rather shaken looking man stood waiting to enter. He glanced towards Frank and did a double take, before suddenly busying himself with his tablet. *Guess I'm famous,* thought Frank with a wry smile. The aide motioned for him to go on alone and, striding out of the elevator, Frank winked at the tall man who was doing his best to ignore him. At the end of a short corridor, Frank pushed a button on the wall next to the only door there. It opened immediately and, with a deep breath, Frank stepped confidently forward to meet his fate.

The room was huge, but Frank immediately spotted Johan Larrouy. The boss of Cyber-Tech had his back to him and was looking out of the giant windows towards the Chicago skyline. Frank suddenly felt wary of the whole situation. Confidence was certainly something Larrouy didn't lack, but to be this casual…

"So, Frank. I suppose you're here to kill me?"

Frank ignored his question, ready with one of his own. "Tell me Larrouy, was it all worth it?" he asked, struggling to control his temper.

The large man turned to face Frank with a broad smile. "In a word Frank, yes"

"Why you…" began Frank, quickly morphing his arms into cannons. On the way here, he'd told himself a hundred times to remain calm. He couldn't afford to lose his cool until he'd heard what Larrouy had to say. Surely the man would find some excuse, some reason why all this was necessary, hell, even someone else to blame. But no, Johan Larrouy was actually proud of what he'd done. Innocent people had suffered because of his need for money and power, and Frank couldn't help but snap. He took aim and fired.

But nothing happened.

Frank then watched in horror as his limbs started to change before his eyes. His arms morphed of their own accord, slowly returning to their normal state despite his desperate attempts to stop it. Try as he might, his Cortex just wasn't responding. Within seconds, his arms had dropped to hang uselessly by his sides and the only thing he could move was his head. *This isn't happening,* he thought desperately. All of his robotics had shut down and he no longer had control. Slowly, Frank began to feel another sensation - fear.

"Yes, sorry about that Frank," said Larrouy holding up a small, black transmitter. "Crawford said this thing would override your Cortex signals and guess what, he was right."

Larrouy began to walk towards Frank, who was just about managing to hold his nerve. He'd been in worse situations than this before, but he just couldn't bring any to mind right now.

"I'm going to let you into a secret, Frank," said Larrouy slowly and still with a smile. "At the start of all this, you were nothing to me, just some part of my granddaughter's pet project. But surviving COLT? Morphing weapons? Well, that changed things pretty quickly. I thought to myself, who better to send to Russia than you? A walking memory stick with unlimited firepower! I needed that data and, somewhat against the odds, you went and got it for me. But you know what Frank, the bit I really like, is just how well you tied up all my loose ends. A suggestion here, a promise there and you played along perfectly. Even Helena got that bit right."

"How could you use your own granddaughter?"

"She knew what she was doing."

"Yes, but you pushed her too far and guess what, now she's after making things right."

"Wrong again, Frank. At this exact moment in time, she's on a jet to England with your friend Harwood. Oh, sorry to break it to you, but he's another ex-Delta on my payroll I'm afraid," finished Larrouy with genuine pride.

Frank tried not to let his surprise show. If Larrouy thought Helena was on a plane, then surely he didn't know what had just happened in Frost's office. Someone here was playing a game of their own. Was it Harwood? Frank didn't think so and that meant his old boss was probably calling the shots. He needed to know more.

"I've spoken to Frost," he began, testing gently.

"Actually, you did more than that didn't you?" said Larrouy with a laugh. "Why do you think I told you about Canagan? I knew he'd eventually lead you to Frost, better still if you had vengeance in mind. That old man did me proud, but he was past it, he needed replacing. Anyway Frank, you should be thanking me," grinned Larrouy. "Killing him, you finally got that revenge you always wanted."

"What if he's not dead?" asked Frank.

"I've had it confirmed by his secretary. Pretty girl that one, and, despite her security clearance, she actually worked for me all along. Sorry Frank, but I needed Frost dead and, given the right push, you went and did it for me."

So, thought Frank, *he doesn't know about Harwood and Helena being there too. But was Frost dead? And what about Harwood? What if he'd recovered enough to overpower Helena?* Once again Frank found himself juggling more questions than answers.

"And so, here we are," said Larrouy, his smile fading. "I'm afraid it's time to die Frank." At that moment there came a knock at the door and Swamps entered, pushing an empty gurney before him. He gave Frank a wide grin.

"Oh and of course we'll be needing our technology back," said Larrouy looking amused.

Frank tried desperately to move, but he was still stuck rigid... except... except for one brief moment he thought he felt a finger twitch. Trying not to be obvious, he experimented with a few slight movements and, to his relief, found he was regaining at least some control. But he needed more time.

"It wasn't just TALIR was it?"

"Of course not. It's taken me a lot of time and money, but I now hold the key to most of the world's terror organizations."

"That key being Delta."

"Indeed," smiled Larrouy.

"But I know Delta, they're good men. How did you get them to do it?"

"What? No guesses, Frank?"

"Money?"

"No, much simpler than that. They were bored and I gave them something to do."

Frank didn't know what to say to that.

"It's really very simple Frank. After the Eastern Wars finally ended, a lot of soldiers found themselves with nothing to do. Worst hit were the elite, soldiers like the SEALS and Delta. What's the point in being highly trained when there's no one to fight? I offered them an opportunity and, after Frost came on board, most of Delta followed suit. Those who didn't were transferred out. It really was that simple."

"Bored soldiers playing at being terrorists," said Frank sadly.

"You know what? I think they actually enjoy it," grinned Larrouy. "But you're probably right; I bet the money helps ease a few guilty consciences too."

"And all of this means more weapons."

"Sure does."

"Escalation," whispered Frank.

"Last year the US government alone ordered over two hundred billion dollars' worth of Cyber-Tech's weaponry," grinned Larrouy. "In February of this year, the senate voted unanimously in favour of continuing the fight against terrorism. I'm pretty sure the bombing of a conference in Lake Tahoe which killed fifteen of them helped smooth the way for that one"

Frank hardly heard him. He was too busy trying to think of a way to stall for more time. "But what about Canagan?" he asked desperately. "Why'd he choose to die?"

"He didn't. Turned out he'd had enough of Delta and wanted to leave. Frost agreed to let him go after this one last job, and then rigged the bomb to go off early."

"Jesus," whispered Frank in shock.

"And now Frost's dead, there's nothing tying me to TALIR. In fact…"

"I didn't kill him!" yelled Frank desperately. "He was alive when I left his office, his secretary lied to you." Although Frank felt back in control of his limbs, he still didn't know if he'd be able to morph his guns.

"You're bluffing," replied Larrouy with a smile.

"Afraid not, Larrouy. When I left Frost he was dying, not dead."

"Well, perhaps you're right Frank. I tell you what, why don't we make a quick call and find out."

"You do that. I've got all day."

Larrouy smiled as he moving towards his desk. "That's funny Frank. But you know what, you've kinda lost me here. I don't get what you hope to achieve..."

"This!" shouted Frank, suddenly bolting forwards. He saw surprise register on the big man's face, which quickly turned to horror as Frank threw his arms around him, picked him up and ran straight at the windows.

Glass shattered, exploding outwards as the two men smashed through the window of Larrouy's penthouse office. Tumbling through the air, Frank held on to Larrouy as the large man desperately struggled to escape his embrace. Exactly what he hoped to achieve by freeing himself, Frank couldn't begin to imagine, but he wasn't going to take that chance. If Frank was going to die, then Johan Larrouy was coming with him.

As he plunged to his doom holding onto the man responsible for TALIR's bloody campaign, Frank found his head start to clear. Anger, pain, revenge... all of these emotions suddenly seemed so trivial. Within him grew an understanding, a realization of the truth behind this state of mind. The reasoning that had affected his judgement, the almost overwhelming desire to kill... to murder those he thought responsible. None of this actually mattered, none of this was the truth. Finally, Frank understood.

His death wouldn't bring Lara and Aayla back.

More importantly, the only way he'd ever be able to treasure their memories, was to let them live on in his heart. The timing could have been better, but Frank had unexpectedly found a reason to live. He had to find a way to turn his back on all of this rage, to leave behind the pain that had been a part of him for so long and move on with his life. Killing Johan

Larrouy simply wasn't the answer.

Decision made and with only seconds left, Frank tried to morph his legs. As he felt the Cortex responding to his instructions, his relief was palpable. When the rocket jets fired up, he whispered a small prayer of thanks to whoever it was up there kind enough to give him a second chance. Touching down gently before the Cyber-Tech building, passers-by looked on in wonder, not least at the sight of Johan Larrouy collapsing to the ground in a dead faint. Frank smiled. For the first time in what seemed like a long, long time, he knew he'd done the right thing. He hadn't been coerced, he hadn't been tricked and he hadn't let anyone else make a decision for him. This was the way it should be and it was a pleasant feeling indeed. Revenge, it seemed, was a poison now leeched from his system.

The sound of approaching police sirens brought further relief, for it surely meant that Helena had made that call and was safe. Indeed, only minutes later uniformed police officers were rushing around to seal off the area. Heavily armed SWAT teams flooded into Cyber-Tech, whilst more surrounded the slowly awakening Larrouy. Frank couldn't help but notice with some satisfaction that he was already in handcuffs.

"Sergeant Reynolds," said an older man, approaching him with a group of aides. Frank smiled at his old commissioner. He'd been one of the good guys.

"I must say Frank," began the commissioner, stopping before him, "that when Dr Brown called, I had a bit of trouble believing her. Turns out Colonel Frost…"

"Frost..." interrupted Frank anxiously, "is he...?"

"He's pretty beat up, but he'll live. Told us enough to confirm what the doctor had said about TALIR and its connections to Larrouy." The commissioner chuckled to himself. "Looks like you've stirred up a hornet's nest Frank."

"He needed stopping."

"Well, I won't argue with that. Look, I'll need a statement from you sometime, you okay with that?"

"Sure, no problem."

"Dr Brown's downtown giving hers right now."

"She okay?"

"She's been through a lot, but she's holding up. In fact, she asked me to give you this," said the commissioner, removing a cell phone from his pocket and passing it to Frank. "Okay, I've got a whole heap of things need to be done; good work bringing Larrouy down, Frank," and with a friendly pat on the back, the older man left him to it.

Frank was still staring at the phone in his hand when it began to ring.

"Hello Frank."

Frank recognized the voice immediately and smiled. "Hey Helena, they still got you down at the station?"

"No, I'm... well, I'm at the airport."

"Jeez, that was quick."

"I need to get away for a while."

"What, no goodbyes?" asked Frank, trying to sound upbeat, but feeling a bit lame. After everything they'd been through together, he'd hoped to perhaps see her again soon.

"Well, I guess this is goodbye Frank and thank you."

"For what?" he asked.

"For not killing him. It must have been…difficult."

"Actually, you know what?" replied Frank with a small smile. "It wasn't that difficult in the end. Anyway, I should be thanking you."

"After what my family's done to you? I don't think…"

"Larrouy had me," said Frank, interrupting her. "All my robotics were all locked up and then, suddenly, I'm free; something you did right?"

"It was just a hunch. I thought he'd try something like that one day, so I made a few changes to your Cortex."

"When? After Russia?"

Frank heard her laugh gently down the line. "Yes, after Russia. After I'd realized a few things about myself. But it was nothing really; all I did was reprogram your Cortex enough to think for itself."

"Well, whatever you did, it saved my life and I'm grateful."

"Look, I've really got to go and, like I said, I just wanted to say thanks, for everything."

"Look after yourself Dr Brown," said Frank and he meant it.

"Goodbye Frank," came the brief reply before the line went dead.

Frank put the phone in his pocket and slowly looked around. *So, what now?* he thought to himself.

What now indeed answered the Cortex.

EPILOGUE

"Well Ms Larrouy, I must say I'm impressed. If the production models are half as good as these prototypes, I reckon your company's in line for the biggest defense contract in history."

"Glad you like them General," replied the smartly-dressed woman. "Johan Larrouy's mistakes nearly destroyed Cyber-Tech, but I intend to take it to new heights."

The Chief of Defense felt a strange unease. In the past, his dealings with Johan Larrouy had been a necessary evil. He'd actively disliked the man and hadn't shed any tears when the traitor was sentenced to be put on death row. But his replacement, well, she was something of an enigma. Despite the vast intelligence network at his disposal, he hadn't been able to unearth much about her and that made him nervous.

"Indeed, the way you've bounced back after TALIR…"

"Is not something I want to discuss," she interrupted firmly.

"Of course," replied the general, not wanting to cause any friction. He was in an unenviable position. Before him was the answer to saving thousands of lives. These new DROLTS were quite unlike any of the automated droids the military had tried before. For a start, they didn't need weapons. They were the weapons. This new morphing technology allowed them to produce a variety of armaments, for a variety of situations. From the viewing platform of Cyber-Tech's vast weapons testing facility, he'd just watched one of the DROLTS changing from a sniper role, to providing an artillery barrage, before finally engaging in close-quarter combat, and all in under a minute. This project could well change the face of the military forever and the smiling Ms Larrouy knew that only too well.

"The COLT project proved that morphing was viable," she continued, "but it was our development of the AI brains that made all this possible. These DROLTS are reliable, loyal and, unlike your regular troops, expendable."

Yes indeed, he thought, *she's got me exactly where she wants me.* "I think we can come to some arrangement Ms Larrouy. I'll have my men work out the details for you."

"Thank you General, it'll be my pleasure," she answered with a dazzling smile before leading him away from the platform.

"Oh, one last thing," he began slowly. "If I was to give you a timescale of, let's say two weeks, how many fully operational DROLTS could you have ready?"

"Well General," replied Pamela Larrouy with a

smile. "That would depend on how many you wanted."

The End

AFTERWORD
THE STORY OF COLT-45

In early 2013, I started work on a comic book story called COLT-45. After a promising start and with a keen artist on board, it soon looked like becoming a reality. But due to some unforeseen circumstances, the project quickly died and that was the end of that.

Or was it?

I still believed the story had potential and so, refusing to be defeated, I decided to have a go at writing COLT-45 in prose form, using the original comic script as a starting point. Besides, I already had a good number of short stories and flash fiction published, so how hard could it be?

As it turned out, very hard indeed.

Only a few months after putting pen to paper, I'd

churned out 25,000 words and COLT-45 was complete. Flushed with success, I immediately submitted my novella to several large publishers and sat back to wait for the royalties. If I recall correctly, the nicest quote I received was *"...reads like a first draft..."* and the rest weren't even that kind. I quickly realised where I'd gone wrong.... it was a first draft! The book was far from complete and as any real author would tell you, getting those initial ideas onto paper is only the first step along the long road to its completion. Downhearted, I was ready to give up on the whole thing, but hidden away within all the criticism I found one really important piece of advice – *"...try employing the services of a Beta Reader..."*

A what? I asked myself, once again showing my naivety. As it turns out, the job of a Beta Reader is (perhaps somewhat unsurprisingly) to read your book. They then offer a range of suggestions for its improvement and so with nothing to lose, I submitted COLT-45 to a small group of professional Beta Readers. Within a few weeks, most of their highly detailed reports had been returned and they all said the same thing...

Start again.

The problem, it seemed, was my style. I'd gone about COLT-45 by simply expanding on what I'd written for the comic, however creating prose is a very different concept. In a comic script, there's no need to describe each panel in minute detail. That's the artist's job and they do it with pictures. But if you leave the description out of a book, it just feels empty.

A reader can't possibly know what's going on in a writer's head, nor do they have any artwork to guide them and so it's up to you to provide that detail. Another mistake I'd made was to jump very quickly from one event to the next, the way the panels in a comic tend to do. Write a book that way and it simply doesn't work, any complex storylines and the reader just gets confused. And so post Beta Reading, I found myself with the following problems: The story needed more action, the characters required development, the dialogue needed an overhaul, the flashbacks didn't make sense and as if that lot wasn't enough, the entire structure of the book needed to be reworked.

So, definitely time to call it a day then?

Now I won't say I wasn't tempted, but I'm not one to give up on things lightly and so began six months of solid re-writes. During that time, it became increasingly obvious that my critics had been right. The changes I undertook not only morphed COLT-45 into something new, they made it into something better. Looking back, I probably did indeed 'start again' as the finished manuscript now bears little resemblance to the original. Eventually I felt confident enough in sending my story to an Editor to be proof read. Not only did Alison Williams polish the writing, but she also suggested several important changes. *Not more re-writes!* As it turned out, these final changes gave new depth to the characters and are now, without doubt, my favourite parts of the book. And so, after one last edit from Alison, COLT-45 was sitting pretty at little over 31,000 words.

Rather like having your third child; you just know when you're done.

It had taken me a full year to re-write COLT-45, but the story was now a very different beast and I'd learnt some valuable lessons along the way. Writing a book isn't just that initial splurge of ideas, quickly followed by periods of boundless enthusiasm, untapped creativity and frenzied writing. Mostly it's a long, tedious and often soul destroying period spent editing, correcting and re-writing that very 'first draft.'

So was it all worth it? Hopefully there's a few people out there who'll enjoy the story and maybe even some who'll appreciate the effort involved. But would I do it all again…?

Well, that's another story.

BIOGRAPHY

Chris Redfern's stories have been published in a wide array of books, magazines and comics. For a full list of prior and upcoming titles, please visit:

www.aatwatchtower.com

12815364R00084

Printed in Poland
by Amazon Fulfillment
Poland Sp. z o.o., Wrocław